The
RAT
Murders

Norman Giddan

Cult Classics Publisher •Dallas, TX

THE RAT MURDERS
By Norman Giddan

Cult Classics Publisher
1613 A Black Duck Terrace
Carrollton, TX 75010
www.cultclassicspublisher.com

ISBN 978-0-9848827-9-3

Book by Lone Star Productions
Contact: ginniebivona@sbcglobal.net

The
RAT
Murders

Chapter One

"I'm Kip. I'm an alcoholic."

The sleepy group nodded. "Hi, Kip."

"I've got some good news and some bad news." His hands twisted around each other and he wiggled his muscular six-foot frame in the narrow folding chair.

He eyed the quirky collection of individuals, seated in fifteen chairs arranged in three rows, dark curtains pulled down, the smoke so thick it could blind a driver on Texas' toll-roads. The aroma of dirty bodies covered by filthy, torn clothes contributed to the groggy malaise. Chocolates and Cokes on a side table, half gone by now, did little to make this Sunday midnight AA meeting in a classroom at the Landing, a homeless shelter, a pleasant experience. Of course, it wasn't supposed to be fun and games.

Kip blew his nose and coughed several times. "The good news is I had been sober ninety-four days, until yesterday that is. The bad news is I've been drunk since then. No food. Slept two hours. I met a woman in a bar who reminded me of Wendy. Fueled my slip big-time." He shut down, head in hands, sobbing a low, slow, sputter of tears.

No one spoke. Several picked up more chocolates and slid back into their chairs. Two old geezers hunched over and snored in the third row. An independent survey would count twelve of fifteen members as regular visitors or frequent inhabitants of the Landing.

Kip looked up. Marty sat in the front row. She remained his loyal partner in their private investigator business. Occasionally, she gave the lead. Tonight was his turn. Two AA folks in the same business, working closely with each other, both ex-cops, violated everything AA taught. She winked at him, then flicked the huge, dangling silver hoops hanging from each ear.

1

Kip said, "I'm ready now. My wife Wendy died of cancer several years ago. It was horrible. I did all I could, but it didn't do it. I failed miserably. So did the doctors at the hospital and the hospice team. She died in my arms. Just up-chucked and shuddered and was gone."

Marty said, "You didn't die. She did. Feel for her, be sad for her."

"It felt like I died," Kip said. "The pain and loss…I drank and drank and drank for about a year. I resigned from the police force. I never took the lieutenant's exam." He pounded the table with both fists. He knew the long thick scar on his neck reddened, as he felt the heat. That peculiar twitch in his left eye came on sporadically, a sign he was pissed-off at himself or someone else or the world.

He stood. The chair creaked. "So, I'm a miserable, fucking drunk who needs a new sponsor I can't bullshit. I need help bad. I'm not a cop anymore but I still carry a gun as a licensed peace office. Get it?"

Kip collapsed, still conscious but nearly delirious.

Marty led him out of the room after two of the regulars helped him onto his feet. "Lean on me. Let's walk a little. Out of this hell-hole," she said. They stumbled down a long hallway and out to the dark street.

He nodded, stretching his arms and shoulders. "I'm okay, now. We need a drink and then…"

"Crap," Marty said. "I'm your partner! Reforming drunk or recovering alcoholic, or whatever…but no booze. Nada. None. Only a six pack of regular Coca-Cola, not diet or zero."

Kip's eye twitched. "There's an old guy in a hoodie following us."

Marty turned slightly. She stopped and peered at the mirror from her purse. "You're right on. Still a damn good cop."

Kip said, "So much shit goes on down here near the Landing."

"Here's my car. Get in," Marty said. He did. She drove without lights. She'd been a cop, too.

Kip turned to eyeball her. "You're still so goddamn beautiful it hurts."

"I'm thirty-five, now," Marty said, "and still a Latino ex-cop who got fed up with our brothers in blue. Too much testosterone and macho bullshit."

"I'm older. I don't care. I love you," Kip said. He touched her shoulder lightly.

She pushed him away. "Down boy, down." She braked hard at the stop sign.

A street guy, bundled up in layers of torn sweaters and coats despite the summer heat banged on the hood. Kip remembered him from AA.

"Stop it," Marty said. "Get away from the car." She honked the horn several times.

The guy blocked the front fender so she couldn't drive. "I need money or wine. Your choice, little lady."

"Get the fuck away or you'll be road kill," Kip said as he got out of the car.

The guy walked away without a word.

"You scared him," Marty said.

"I'm a drunk ex-cop who could have beaten the shit out of him." Kip sat down, trying to control the shakes.

"If you could stand," Marty said.

"It sounds crazy, but I want to do something for these homeless fuckers," Kip said. "Most of them at the Landing are fucked up. I'll volunteer someday. I'm not just another fed-up citizen who doesn't give a rat's ass."

"It might help you, too." Marty said. "If you stopped the booze, it would be a good thing. What's that stuff about being a friend in order to have a friend?"

Kip said, "Here's a theory. Do good for others and it'll be good for you." He slid down into the seat, fast asleep.

At the rental duplex they shared, Marty lifted, then carried, and finally dragged Kip to his door. "Nighty night, boss. See you ma-ñana for coffee. We've got a PI offer to discuss and plan. We've got a fucking good offer from the Police-FBI Joint Task Force. Some asshole who worked at several non-profit agencies is sus-pected of theft."

Kip inched open his door, slipped to the floor, then slept with

3

the door slightly ajar. A small, white, silk banner hung on the inside of the door blew in the slight breeze. It read "Your Higher Power."

He awakened suddenly around 4:00 a.m., mind foggy and horribly thirsty. Three glasses of ice water re-kindled his high, so he made a pot of coffee. After two cups of black, laced with three teaspoons of sugar, he locked the door and plopped fully clothed onto his bed. The phone woke him again around 8:00 a.m.

Marty said, "Get ready. I'll bring in donuts and coffee and orange juice. Then we can talk PI. Okay?"

Kip said, "Yes. I'll brush my teeth. Even though I'm almost forty, I still brush twice a day, but only floss once."

Marty knocked on the door a half-hour later, armed with a huge shopping bag. She poured coffee and juice and laid out a dozen cake donuts coated with chocolate icing.

He said, "Thanks." He spilled OJ on his new red running shorts, and shaking slightly, wiped it off.

"They want us. They want us now," Marty said. She dunked an old-fashioned into coffee. It broke off and floated.

"Why don't they use their own cops or agents? Christ, the Task Force is loaded."

Marty poured more coffee for both of them. "Their story is that they want it very low profile, without the FBI or local police doing it. No big deal, just routine, so they'll outsource it to us—two lowly PIs."

Wearing tight jeans and black boots, Marty waltzed around the room, which was horribly decorated with stick furniture and discarded half-empty pizza boxes and beer bottles. The odor was faintly like the inside of a garbage can. "Reg, the FBI guy, told me that there's suspicion about the current director at the Landing, a guy they all call Dock. Nothing solid," Marty said.

"Ho! Ho! Dock at the Landing," Kip said.

"He's apparently clean but problems surfaced at the St. Francis Kitchen of the Poor when he worked there."

"What kind?" Kip asked.

Marty said, "A shit load of missing valuable food at St. Francis and then money at Sally's. So, we go there, talk to people. You know, we ask questions and they pay us whether we find anything conclusive or not."

"Love our government," Kip said. Now he danced in a circle while he held both of Marty's hands. "Sweet. Is it too early for vodka and burgers?"

"Go get cleaned up and we're on our way. This place stinks," she said. "I'll wait outside. I could clean it up but I'd only enable you. Ha! Ha!"

Kip shaved slowly so he could maintain the outline of his beard. He recalled being an MP in Iraq. His squad entered a dusty, small, outlying village to investigate whether the local chief was stealing grain from the mud storage sheds. As squad leader, Kip sent two men to serve as lookouts while he entered the village leader's house with the other three. Several women and children huddled near a wood stove in the kitchen area, and three men squatted on patterned, colorful rugs in the main living area drinking tea. An Iraqi jerked a pistol from under his robes and shot a soldier in the leg. Kip's squad quickly killed them, even shot a woman who screamed as she jumped into the fray.

Kip felt uncertain, confused about what had happened, and mixed-up about who he was and what he should be. With a black military father and a white mother, he thought of himself as a mutt, part this and part that. Kids at school teased and taunted him about his light cocoa-colored skin. His family moved to so many bases that he lost count by high school. He brother came along and was a darker brown.

Kip, out of sync with traditional American values, didn't fully support the military intervention in the Middle East. Yet, he found himself fighting in Iraq, being shot at, bombed in his Humvee, and finally ambushed by Al-Qaeda insurgents. As an African-American soldier originally trained as an MP, but now going out daily on search-and-destroy missions, shooting at other non-whites who were horribly poor and uneducated, he failed to resolve his fragmented identity, a reluctant soldier trying to follow in his father's footsteps, never sure it was the right thing for him.

The razor caught on a piece of skin. Kip stopped the bleeding from a small cut on his lip. His hand shook as he vomited breakfast into the small sink. "Now, I'm ready."

Their business, Crandall and Flores PI, barely survived from month-to-month, "hand-to-month" as Kip put it. They shared an old dented maroon Ford sedan with mismatched hubcaps and four bald tires.

"If we go to St. Francis first, we can nose around, ask some questions, maybe be invited for lunch," Kip said. His hand skimmed his brush-cut.

"That's what I like about you. Be prepared. A genuine Boy Scout," Marty said. She drove slowly, the sedan's choice, through an aging southern section full of crumbling brick buildings and boarded-up storefronts.

Kip marveled at the gleaming, shiny skyscrapers in the Dallas foreground, maybe two miles away to the north. St. Francis must have been hallowed ground in its day, a towering Gothic church with high spires, and several carved Biblical figures on either side of the huge, grey-stone entrance. Two smaller side buildings housed the soup kitchen and an elementary school with its own basketball floor.

As they approached it, a sign on one of the two-story buildings read "Hope is Here." Unexpectedly, a young, handsome priest greeted them as they arrived. "It's early for lunch. I'm Father O'Neill." He waved them in.

"How do you do, Father? Nice to meet you." They shook hands. "I'm Kip Crandall and this is Marty Flores. We're PIs hired to do some routine background work for a cold case. Like outsourcing."

Marty said, "Nothing big-time. Glad to meet you, Father." She eyed the short man.

"Please come in. We'll have coffee and talk." He pointed to a table. "We can sit here. Lunch won't be served for an hour or so. Better watch out then, they storm in here starved and thirsty. We serve hope and love here, disguised as bologna sandwiches and hot soup." A cherubic smile crossed his pink-cheeked face, topped by neatly trimmed, premature salt and pepper hair.

Kip asked, "Father, were you here when a truckload of fruit and veggies went missing? Maybe a year or so ago."

"Oh, yes. I recall the incident very well. We get deliveries early in the morning, usually around 4:00 a.m. The farmer's market folks charge us a very reasonable price." He poured coffee. "Here's sugar and thick yellow cream. The men like real old-fashioned cream. And plenty of sugar—too much of it.

"So the truck arrived early one morning and two cooks unloaded several crates of vegetables for a soup that day. The driver came into the kitchen to smoke a cigarette with his coffee."

"Anything unusual?" Marty asked.

Father O'Neill said, "Yes, when he went outside to drive to his next delivery the truck was not there. Simply gone. Happened in just ten or fifteen minutes." He pulled on his collar.

Kip said, "And that's it? Thousands of dollars of veggies and fruit stolen in a flash?"

"Exactly. Our head chef called 911 and the police but the truck wasn't located until the next day. Miles away and burned out." Father O'Neill poured more coffee and replenished the creamer.

Marty said, "Thank you, Father, it's delicious. By the way, the chef wasn't called Dock, was he?"

"You've evidently seen the reports. Yes, he was. Very nice man and a good cook, too." The priest loosened his collar, revealing a red rash.

As they arose from the table, Kip stretched his legs, and stood tall to tighten his core. They were finished with the coffee and the story, so far. "May we see the kitchen?" Kip asked.

"But of course. Follow me." He rubbed his neck. "The police suspected an inside job, so to speak, but their interrogation yielded nothing solid. The truck driver apparently knew Dock and several other kitchen workers. They lived in the same rooming house. All denied being complicit in the theft. We have complete faith and trust in the truthfulness of our staff."

The three of them walked through the large but outdated kitchen area—huge chipped, white freezer, dark brown ovens and a blackened gas stove with eight greasy burners. The air was fifty-percent Lysol. A side door led to an alley where the truck had parked.

"Very convenient," Marty said. "Neat location for a heist."

"We'll need to talk to the truck driver, of course," Kip said.

Father O'Neill said, "Won't be possible. He left town after the incident and this fellow Dock took a better job with the Salvation Army. The police had no solid evidence to arrest or charge…"

"Come on now, Father," Kip said. "Looks mighty fishy to me. And it's not even Friday." His eye twitched slightly.

"Stop it, Kip. You didn't push it very hard, did you, Father O'Neill?" Marty asked.

"Well," Father said, "I guess not. Dock's record here was spotless and the driver couldn't be found. Of course, their prints were everywhere as we would expect."

Kip said, "What about justice? You didn't want it known that thieves and crooks worked here. Is that it?"

"Yes, I suppose so." Father O'Neill led the way to the front door.

"You don't want us to question anyone else, do you?" Kip said. He leaned down to tie his shoelaces.

"No, I suppose not. Insurance paid for the truck and the Diocese paid one-half of the several thousands of dollars of stolen food. Goodbye."

Kip said, "Thank you for your time."

Seated in their car again, Marty said, "They're good at that."

"Cover-ups?" Kip asked.

"Yes, I suppose so." She twisted the silver bangles hanging from her ears. "He sure looked me over. Just like you do. Stop it."

"You're prejudiced. You hate priests," Kip said.

"Not all of them."

"You were just a kid, weren't you? Priest knocked you up. He made you give it away," Kip said. "That even makes me hate them—but not all of them."

"They behave like cops. No snitches. No squealers. They always have each other's backsides. They protect each other. Fierce loyalty. No rats. Cover-up shit-piles, just like cops do. That's the good side."

Kip pounded the steering wheel. His eye twitched furiously this time. "The bad side is what some of them do to young boys and nuns. And then lie about it. And what they do to young girls. And then lie about it. Oh, good Father, let me send you to another church, or a different city, or out of the country. They've ruined plenty of lives." His scar became hot and thick. His index finger outlined the bulging knife wound.

Marty said, "Salvation Army is supposedly the next stop. Maybe we'll have better luck. Their main store is not far from here. Much of the low-end stuff is in the southern area."

"If we ask questions and look around, we can stretch it out to a full day's pay," Kip said. "I forgot lunch. I've got this rust-bucket floored. It's only going forty-two MPH."

Marty said, "Slow down, boss. Car's got a mind of its own."

"There it is," Kip said. "It's huge. Was a supermarket. Then a gospel church. Now it's the Salvation Army. Competes head-on with Goodwill and St. Vincent de Paul."

Their car blended in perfectly with the paint-stained sedans, whose cracked windows and dented fenders crowded the parking lot.

Kip's cell rang. "Yes, morning, Reg." He shifted the phone to speaker.

Reg, who ran the forensics lab at FBI in Dallas, their current employer, said, "We've got more serious rumors about the head of that homeless place. Don't forget that he was at the Salvation Army when money went missing."

Kip said, "Any evidence tracing it to Dock?"

"Not really," Reg said. "You can see the reports. You or Marty could investigate in person, but I don't want to do anything to queer the deal. Very low key, so just use the phone."

Marty said, "I'll just make a friendly call." On speaker phone she dialed the Salvation Army Resale Shop and asked for the manager.

"This is Colonel Schultz."

"Hello, Colonel Schultz, I'm Marty Flores a private investigator. Wanted to ask you a question or two, if that's all right with you." She floated on numerous pillows used to raise the dilapidated passenger seat.

"I guess it's okay."

"We wanted to follow-up on that theft of cash at Christmas. It

9

was $900, I believe."

"Oh, yes ma'am, that was it. No one knows anything. Just disappeared from a kettle brought to the office." He coughed authoritatively. "Police have been on it."

"Yes, sir, just wondered if any new information surfaced. It's happened in other cities and states. Same kind of thing—never more than $1,000 or so." With a weak and excessively polite voice, she deflected suspicion and reduced any natural defensiveness. "So, it's not really any individual staff member's fault."

"Of course, of course, Ms. Flores. No new evidence. Police interrogated all my employees, even those from our food service. No luck. Of course, I've got my hunches about..."

"Yes," she said and sat upright. "Go, on."

"Well now, this is off-the-record, but the kitchen and cook staff were kind of slippery, not as trustworthy as the repair and sales folks here in the store. I've almost got the feeling several have served prison time. We give everyone a second or third chance. This is God's army."

"Thank you, sir. If anything else comes up, please call me at 214-731-8767. It's Marty Flores. Thanks again."

Out came the black faux leather notebook. She wrote "possible suspicion" at Salvation Army. No evidence. No proof. Probably not worth visiting.

Kip called Reg on the speaker phone. "Maybe Dock got away with some stuff, maybe he didn't. If he's smart, he won't try again very soon. Marty got nothing solid over the phone."

Reg said, "Thanks. You guys did good."

Kip said, "Just because it happened while he was at those places, doesn't mean he did it, or even knew about it. We've got to be fair."

"You're right. Dock's personal and work record are very good. Keep your eyes and ears open," Reg said. He hung up.

Marty said, "Not your pants."

"Very funny," Kip said. "By the way, I'm already a little paranoid about this Dock guy. Of course, we're only outsourcing contract work for the FBI." He couldn't hold back a sarcastic bellylaugh. "Nobody fucks with the Bureau or our sister, the Secret

Service. Between us we nearly got Reagan killed, after we got Kennedy shot. Then there was Ford."

"Both President Bushes are still alive," Marty said.

Chapter Two

Dock rubbed his strong hands together, washing the blood from them into the large, rusted, metal sink of the Landing's kitchen. The watery, red droplets slowly dripped into the drain. He'd saved a life.

His mind reeled with the events of the last hour. He behaved like a good hands-on administrator that night, prowling the center's halls, a smile here, a handshake there, apparently working and helpful. As he limped by a conference room, a huge black man called Enuf-el, a former pro football lineman his friends said, and two drunken homeless shelter regulars argued over the score of a Super Bowl game of seven or eight years ago.

Enuf-el said he was right because he had played in the game. The two other men claimed to be correct since they'd watched it together in a bar in Hoboken, New Jersey. The brawl erupted after Enuf-el said, "You two faggots don't know shit! I was in it, motherfuckers!"

When they jumped him, he struggled into the hallway near the crowded living room wallpapered with huge flat-screen TVs. A voice screamed, "Turn off those fucking Oprah re-runs. She ain't like us."

Neatly dressed in jeans and a heavily starched white shirt, Dock innocently limped by, an unplanned visit to a brutal fight like he'd had in prison. The smaller guys strapped Enuf-el's massive arms to his sides, then smashed in his nose and beat him with the broken arm from an old club chair. Enuf-el recovered, jerked his arms loose, grabbed their heads and banged them together. Hard enough for serious concussions. Even with helmets and pads this would have been a very rough fight, deserving of fines and suspensions in pro football.

Dock yanked one guy off of the football player and slugged the second one in the gut. Breathless and heavy-legged, number two fell to the ground. Enuf-el squeezed the throat of number one so hard that a hissing sound emerged. Number two slowly arose, then stood and yelled, "You fucker," while he stuck a fork into Enuf-el's throat. Dock grabbed a towel from a nearby laundry cart, held it tightly on the spurting blood as the two attackers ran for the street. He yelled, "Someone call 911!"

Enuf-el fell over slowly, huge mounds of muscle and bone and fat spilling to the floor—maybe 350 pounds of manhood, in shock and bleeding to death from a fork in his throat.

Dock whispered, "Just like prison. I ought to let him die."

EMT's responded quickly. They told Dock that their truck could have found the way by itself, since so many emergency calls for fighting and drunkenness came from the Landing. Once they stabilized Enuf-el, it took all the strength of two of them to raise his stretcher into the back of the truck.

Dock iced the pain in his throbbing hand. Vigilance at all times. He'd violated the homeless mantra, "Don't help out when there's trouble." It had a street-smart logic to it.

When a police cruiser arrived, he updated the sergeant in charge, cops could chase down the other two fighters, arrest them, and then interrogate Enuf-el in the hospital.

Dock idealized the Landing as a refuge for the needy, the addicts, alcoholics, criminals, the jobless as well as those simply down-on-their-luck for several years. Originally housed in an abandoned red-brick industrial building, it recently moved to a modern three-story location on the edge of downtown Dallas. Such centers, or their supportive housing units, usually overrun by clients, now took on many of the characteristics not only of jails, but of rehab centers and hospitals. Job training, language skills, GED courses, counseling, and financial planning were put on the shelf. Hopefully the perfect place to hide his past.

Dock, full name, Dr. Ralph Meade, appeared on the scene one hot day as if from heaven, and took command after an unusually quick appointment to be the director. With a good job record and no criminal history in Texas, he'd worked in two local soup kitchens. Most of his early background remained a mystery to staff and the inhabitants, yet that apparently didn't matter. Dock described himself as the proverbial light at the end of the jetty. A wise resident joked that the light in question came from an on-coming speedboat about to crash and burn.

As the director, Dock's professional preoccupation, and that of the Landing's staff and clientele turned explicitly to food and shelter—survival. Frequent electricity brown-outs, filthy bath-room sinks over-used for washing when showers broke down, beds without sheets or pillows, and cross-legged homeless seated on the floor of the dining hall due to crowding served to remind the homeless of their plight, as if they needed it. Only a delusion-al few believed that the outside world didn't have it much better.

Of course, he realized that nearly everything was worse for the homeless. When it rained they were soaked, when it snowed they were ice cold, when they arrived at a shelter the odors were hor-rifying. Petty crime was everywhere, safety and comfort was at a premium. The heat and humidity inside the Landing for much of the year stupefied the residents, literally drugging them into a semi-conscious state.

Dock's volunteers actively participated in most activities and programs, even led several of them. Tony and Rocco were his pride and joy. He discussed business with them early the next morning seated around the kitchen's butcher-block table.

Tony applauded, and said, "Well, well, our hero. They saved that black guy at the hospital."

Tony Syzmanski stood six feet tall and three feet wide, weigh-ing in at three hundred pounds. He worked out daily with weights so he blamed the obesity on his genes. "Men are big in my fam-ily." Tony, a volunteer chef and cook, literally ran the kitchen, controlled the flow of food, the choices and the paid staff's activi-ties.

Dock said, "You fat shit, where's the sugar?"

"Look, I'm your volunteer chef and cook, but I don't make cof-fee. I run the place." He stirred a huge cauldron of white potatoes, alone with his memories of grander days. Then he closed the lid on the pot. He liked to show up early.

Rocco said, "Tell us about Denty. Come on, shithead, do it." He peered out of small, grey eyes under a low brow.

15

Tony flexed his huge biceps and lats. Mr. World.

"Denty smiled at me and yelled from the doorway, 'Hey, Tony!' She's still got some appeal at age forty-one! Even washed out from all that crap, abuse, drugs, divorceand booze.

"I said, 'Not open yet.'

"'I want a steak,' she said.

"I stirred the potatoes and turned down the burner. 'A steak, my ass,' I tell her. 'Get out of here, you dumb bitch. Out.' I even shook a ladle toward her several times. Here she comes. She licks her lips. She tip-toes within inches. 'I want a steak. It's been a long time.' She smiles again, her green eyes bloodshot and moist as she moves close to me. She grabs my crotch real tight, digging deep.

"I ask her, 'Jesus, Denty, what are you doing?'"

Dock said, "Get to the bottom line."

"Don't hurry, I like it," Rocco said. He flexed his pecs and smoothed his thick, dark hair.

"'Make me a steak,' she says again.

"Okay, okay, you want a rib-eye or T-bone?

"She squeezes tighter and said, 'There's enough bone here.'

"So I turned off the burner. I pulled her into the stand-up freezer and yanked down her jeans. Then I jerked her long-johns away and off came several layers of panties and underwear." Tony shoved his index finger in and out of his mouth.

"She laughed. 'Takes too long,' she said and dropped my apron to the floor, unzipped my fly and went to work. 'Always like a slurpie with my steak,' she said.

"Broiled or fried? I said. She said, 'Your choice, Tony. You're the cook. Me, I'm just a lowly homeless woman trying to get along in life. I showered this morning.' She smelled her pits.

"'So did I. So did I. So did I.' I sank to my knees, my face bent out of shape. 'Do you want a towel? Is that ooze from your dentures?'

"'I want a steak. Fuck your questions,' she said. She coughed and spit into my apron."

Dock said, "Good story, Tony. Hope she keeps her mouth shut."

Rocco said, "Very funny, Dock." A forty-year-old man, he functioned as the senior volunteer in social services. His task was recruitment of residents, who knew him as the Irish Dago from the Landing. He said, "The guys are sick of the bologna sandwiches. Can't we get dry Genoa salami or some good fat Italian ham?"

Tony said, "Where the fuck you think you are, a rich farmhouse in Tuscany? Forget about it."

"How about some sliced cheese?"

"Oh, sure," Tony said. "Maybe Parmigiano Reggiano."

Rocco laughed, his gaze fixed on Tony's crotch. "Your pants are still open, asshole."

Dock said, "Denty had a visit. She wanted a steak. Did you forget, Rocco?"

Rocco nudged Tony. He slipped into a mock boxer's stance. "You promised me that steak. You fucking traitor."

Tony feigned anger with a wide-eyed grimace and raised his voice. "She treats me good."

Rocco doubled up laughing. His powerfully built frame shook hard. "It's supposed to be high in protein."

Dock said, "Of course, we wouldn't know personally. I've got to go to my office. Somebody has to work in this place."

Dock nurtured a tiny core group of special volunteers, like Tony and Rocco, who participated daily in the programs and services of the center. A second group of more traditional volunteers raised money, handled on-site visits and arranged community relations. Mostly rich and concerned, these latter citizens respected Dock but did not have much of a personal relationship with him. Known to be a widower, Dock constantly fought off the efforts of the female volunteers to find him a wife.

That evening the three of them met in Dock's office for drinks and more talk. Rye and water, no ice, pleased them as the drug of choice. They compared notes, bragged, lied, manipulated, and each opened up just enough to tantalize the other two. Still, plenty of fun keeping dark secrets.

Dock said, "Let's throw down a few before we feed the flock? I need to know you guys better."

"How did you hurt your leg? You limp," Tony said.

"I got stuck in the leg one night when I tried to stop a fight in a bar. They sewed it up, but must have hit a tendon or ligament cause I've never been the same since." Dock said.

Tony said, "Me, I just got fat. Here's some pastrami on bagels with hot mustard and coleslaw." He set the tray on Dock's desk.

"Perfect," Rocco said. "I'll pour us another round."

Dock chug-a-lugged. "Lots of stress here. We're all Catholics, but different. I've got advanced degrees, but Tony, you dropped out of high school, and…?"

"I did a year of community college," Rocco said.

Dock bit into his sandwich. "Delicious, Tony. Thanks. Are you guys sure you're retired businessmen?"

Rocco and Tony gulped their drinks, evading Dock's gaze.

Tony said, "We're different. I'm Polish and Rocco's Italian. You're fucking Irish, Dock. We're real different."

Dock said, "That's not what I asked. You've both got secrets. So do I. I suspect we've all known tough times, even the cruel hand of the law."

"Amen," Rocco said.

Tony nodded.

Dock said, "When I was about fifteen or so, I wanted to join a gang. Mostly brown and black guys—and they wanted me. I would have been the first white guy in it. I hid my good grades in school and aspirations for college from them, tried to act and talk tough with street cred. Somehow, my folks found out about it, just as I was going to have a gang tattoo, a bleeding dragon with a cross, done on my shoulder and back. My dad blew his cork. 'Jesus Christ, did I raise a son to be a gang-banger with a body full of ink? Might as well have had three daughters.' My mother took my side and got me to promise not to join a gang until I was twenty-one. I lied. My dad finally died."

After a few drinks Dock said, "Let's go help."

The three of them climbed into the front bench seat of a small, converted ice cream van. It featured a large roll-up side window and a convenient but narrow serving-table area that hung on two steel cables below the window. A fridge, table, cutting board, coffee maker, bowls of sugar and dry artificial cream, cups, radio, and tiny TV completed the inside kitchen. The ancient hot plate had burned out weeks ago.

Dock suggested that yellow mustard spice up the sandwiches, since mayo spoiled quickly. Homeless people traded fresh food for pills or booze or tobacco, so refrigeration was not exactly typical in their lives. Others stole a bag of ice from a convenience store, necessary for a Jack & Coke, for example, or to chill a cup of Thunderbird wine.

They drove to a homeless encampment near a viaduct, parking close by, Tony walked around the front of the van and came up to a large corrugated metal box.

"You want food?" He asked. "Hungry tonight?"

A raspy Southern voice echoed from inside the box. "No, thank you, sir. I sure would like a drink, though. Help me sleep some."

Tony said, "How's hot coffee? Cream and sugar?"

Out popped a bearded, grizzled old-timer named Buster, head first, slithering on his haunches, feet encased in three or four pairs of socks in varied states of disrepair. "Sure you don't have just a little red wine? Doctor says I've got sleep ap, something or other. It's just too hot to sleep."

Tony said, "Cream or sugar?"

"Yes," Buster said. "Especially the sugar. Maybe a couple of those bologna sandwiches on white bread for breakfast later. Or pate foie gras, if you've got it."

Tony smiled. "Haven't even got no hogshead cheese."

Buster rose on his stocking feet, just over five feet tall. He reached with a rough, grimy hand ending in long, dirty fingernails.

Tony gave him several sandwiches and the hot coffee. "Sorry, no napkins." They both chuckled.

Tony and Rocco rolled on. Dock kept notes on a brief evaluation form used for special volunteers at the center. He liked the feeding program, especially for those who never would stand on their own two feet.

Rocco's flashlight beam burned Queenie's eyes as he approached a low slung tent at the rear of the camp.

"Anyone need a ride? Hospital, jail, the Landing, AA meeting?"

Queenie said, "Very funny, you asshole." She was over six feet tall.

Denty stuck her head out of the tent and put a finger in her mouth pretending to suck on it. "Ever seen a finger come?"

Rocco handed her two sandwiches and a large container of steaming coffee. "You're so athletic, Denty."

"Just ask Tony," she said. "Ask that mother fucker. He'll tell you. I like steak a hell of a lot better than bologna. Makes him harder and me stronger. I like it that way."

Queenie said, "Oh, shut up, Denty. Beggars can't be choosers. Slow night on the streets. Only two Johns. Give me coffee."

Rocco rolled his eyes as he walked away. "You're welcome, ladies. I'd piss my pants if you said 'thank-you'."

Dock dozed in the van. A brief sprinkle of rain blotted out some of the stink from the garbage and filth of this homeless encampment. Frequent heavy rains in the spring forced the tiny stream nearby over its banks, increasing the spread of urban decay floating under the bridge—needles, bottles, tobacco, blood, syringes, condoms, excrement, bones, clothes, useless appliances, even the skeleton of a burned-out, four-door sedan. No corpses were found in it during a brief search by the cops. The city took no action to remove the wreck.

They delivered the last of the food and coffee. Tony and Rocco and Dock sat shoulder-to-shoulder.

Tony said, "Feels good to do it. Real good."

"Yeah," Rocco said. "Not one asshole said thanks. They'd cut off our balls for a few hits of ..."

"I'd hate being homeless," Tony said. "Of course, we've got our own kind of bullshit."

Dock said, "Couldn't agree more." He smoothed his hair and rubbed his baby blues. "I'm beat."

Rocco said, "Shit, I miss my pigeons and I miss gambling in Atlantic City. Gone with the wind." He closed his eyes.

Dock said, "You both did a good job tonight, helpful with a sense of humor. You talk at their level, which is good. Not very hard for either of you, is it?" He knew neither would answer.

As Tony parked the van, Dock noticed a youngster, Tottie, seated on the curb. He said, "You're out kind of late, especially for a ten-year-old, aren't you?" The child feigned a loud snore, shut his eyes, at the same time twirling the basketball he held between his legs.

Tottie said, "Some gangs want a kid like me to join them and do sex. Then I get a bunch of ink. Then I steal a bunch of stuff. Nothing new for me." He smiled with that sweet, bewitching twinkle in his dark eyes. "What I want is a net for the hoop in the parking lot. Like Mike."

"I'll try to put it in the budget. Get some sleep."

Dock returned to his apartment, had a drink, and fell asleep on the couch, exhausted after the evening sojourn of delivering food and coffee. He slept until late morning. Around 4:00 p.m. that afternoon he rode with Rocco to "pick up the ladies" as he euphemistically termed it.

Rocco said, "This dented three-year-old orange piece of shit. I used to have a new BMW with black leather seats every year. Got to conserve in retirement."

Dock admired the shimmering green and blue glass towers in downtown Dallas. Frequent city budget cuts forced downtown plazas to lose their bubbly waterfalls and attractive fountains. It seldom rained and the hot air dried out the colorful boxed plantings and overhanging trees. Replacement cacti provided a small degree of pleasant aesthetics for local shopkeepers and businesses. A losing battle, to be sure, but he was familiar with that kind of fight.

Dock didn't feel comfortable in the semi-industrial area on the edge of downtown, plenty seedy, which served as the location of the Landing. Cleverly positioned, the homeless inhabitants here maintained access to cheap liquor stores, street drug dealers, huge middle-class apartment buildings ripe for second-story robberies, cars with goodies to steal and sell, bridges and overpasses chockfull of space to camp, with or without a tent, a blanket, or a tarp. A local trucker, next door to the center, kept a row of barbed wire on top of an electrified fence to keep out the street people.

Was the Landing located near any businesses or offices that might be offended by a bevy of panhandlers in their midst? Absolutely no! Were these very same businesses and corporate offices willing to donate money to keep the center's clients out of the mainstream of downtown? Absolutely yes! Despite such precautions, "petty crime" near the center committed by street people and the homeless escalated quickly as the economic climate deteriorated. Dock knew there was no increase in felonies, rapes, or murders.

Rocco said, "Look at those three school girls in high white socks and short plaid skirts." He almost rammed the car in front of him. He screeched to a stop but they were gone. After two more blocks and a right turn he swung into the Kitty Kat parking lot.

Their two wives posed outside, both smoking up a storm. Dock admired Tony's wife Teri, dressed in white skin-tight Capri pants and a black bikini bra. She stubbed out her cigarette with three inch heels tied by black straps. Dock loved her tramp stamp of two eagles fucking.

Dock knew about Rocco and Teri, but said nothing. Rocco's own Maryanne was brilliant but quite plain, and Dock needed Tony and Rocco for other ventures.

"There it is," Dock said. "The girls' home away from home." The Kitty Kat sold sex and booze five minutes from the Landing, a perfect spot for the two wives of center-volunteer husbands. Dock had a few drinks there occasionally. Teri danced on a pole and really got down to business in a black sequined g-string. One hand on some guy's open fly, and the other stuffing dollar bills into her g-string, she forced a grin of gratitude.

Maryanne sang her heart out, with and without the questionable aid of a blind drummer, an eighty-year-old cornet player, and a disabled woman fingering a keyboard, frequently out of tune. Her specialty was Broadway hits. Oklahoma and Guys and Dolls ditties. She unbuttoned her blouse provocatively and wore very short skirts. Still sexiness eluded her. Daylight action in the Kitty Kat included retirees, homeless, as well as college students with nothing else to do except study.

The women slithered into the back seat. Dock smiled and said, "Hey."

Teri said, "Tips were shit. Only made eighty bucks." She lit a cigarette and blew smoke at her counter-part.

Maryanne said, "Not too bad for tits and ass. I got fifty for singing, a real talent. Blow that smoke up your ass."

Rocco said, "Please, girls. Not today. Maybe we can grab a bite. Some pasta or something when Tony gets off. Okay?"

Silence.

Dock said, "So it's decided. It's Little Sicily for a pasta dindin." He coughed and sneezed, then rolled down his window.

Teri said, "Better stop them cigars again, Rocco, or you're going to get ED."

Rocco steered the sedan back to the center's parking lot, starting to fill up with folks hungry for a hot meal and a chance to sleep in the open-air plaza. Tony's steaming pots of potatoes, rice, pasta, and the cornbread with tube steak would fill their bellies.

Tony appeared, a tall white cook's hat perched on his huge head. He turned to go back inside, instead tossing the hat through the open kitchen door. As he entered the car, he said, "Goddamn crazy motherfuckers drive me crazy as shit. I need a drink. Those old scars on my back itch like shit. Heat's terrible but in that fucking kitchen it's like the inside of…"

Dock said, "Let's go eat. My treat."

They dropped Dock at his apartment after dinner. He slept fitfully. Too much pasta with marinara sauce, a huge T-bone steak and half a bottle of red table wine.

Mid-morning of the next day he invited both Tony and Rocco into his office. He said, "I need to see both of you today."

A little while later, Rocco and Tony knocked on the office door and entered. Tony said, "It's five o'clock somewhere in this fucking world," when Dock offered them chairs along with double rye and water.

Dock said, "You know I like you guys. We share a lot. But you can't mess so much with these people."

Tony stood and pushed his chair away with a swipe. "Fuck you, Dock. What are you, the school principal?"

Rocco said, "We joke with them. Not much else."

Dock said, "That's not the issue. Denty tells everyone that Tony's fucking her in exchange for gifts. And Buster says he polished Rocco's car for a jug of wine."

Rocco said, "Big fucking deal. Tony gets horny in the kitchen."

"And besides, she blew me," Tony said. He patted his crotch lovingly.

Dock said, "What's with you two? You do a good job for the Landing. I'm pleased. You're not really successful retired businessmen, are you? I'm never sure I can trust you. You're rough guys. Wise guys. Tough guys."

Rocco said, "Why should we trust you, Dock? You'll use stuff on us. Who are you?" He jiggled a gold chain and cross at his neck, which buried itself in heavy matted chest hair.

Dock said, "My dad, a sales manager, well, he did the same stuff as you, Tony. He had numerous affairs and wasn't very careful about who knew his routine. My sisters and I knew, almost from the start. In common psych jargon, he selfishly acted out his sexual needs in a hurtful way. He hurt his wife and his children, and didn't really care about the other women. He drank and lied, but that's another story. He was a fucking rat during their divorce. I still cared about him, but we moved so often and he let my sisters and mother dominate him at home."

Tony said, "You know, there are rumors about you too, Dock. Did you always have blue eyes and blond hair?" He abruptly sat down again.

Dock said, "My work record is spotless."

"You're a big strong guy but I heard the fucking Ph.D. was phony," Rocco said, "from a diploma-mill. Ten grand and one week in California."

"We've certainly got our suspicions about each other," Dock said. "We'd better 'let sleeping dogs lie.' There are ways we can work together and make a lot of money." He raised his glass in a toast. "To us…"

Chapter Three

Kip and Marty felt lucky when recruited by the FBI as a supervising "contract" team in the Witness Protection Program, WPP, to monitor individuals and families in North Texas. Kip learned that two couples from the east coast, Rocco and Maryanne O'Connor and Tony and Teri Syzmanski, joined a dozen other participants. Coincidentally, Tony and Rocco called the Landing their "home away from home away from home," while, to the chagrin of WPP, their wives worked at a nearby topless joint.

Kip (legally Kendrick Franklin Crandall in the FBI contract) wanted both Marty and himself to look sharp now. He dwarfed Marty with his six foot frame and heavily muscled body. Down thirty pounds since his wife's death three years earlier, booze kept him from dropping by fifty. He couldn't take his gaze off of Marty's dazzling Latino beauty, her huge dark eyes, lustrous long hair and sexy demeanor awed him.

Kip still loved her, but she now nurtured a lifetime commitment to her wife, Professor Barbara LeFevre, who worked at the Detroit community college department of English. Marty gave up being a cop after fighting a false allegation of sexually assaulting a female prisoner. Perps knew she was gay and tried to exploit it.

Their low-profile, not altogether successful careers as private investigators, preceded the investigation work for Reg. He liked them and their style. A perfect match with WPP, trained years ago as police officers, but not FBI agents, they were relative strangers in crime prevention, or conduct circles in Dallas.

Simple, straightforward tasks fell their way. Make sure the WPP worked smoothly and that all sides followed their contracts and moral agreements. Sort of probation officers for thugs, thieves, crooks, even killers and their spouses or partners. The FBI told Kip that it arranged for expenses as well as part-time or full-time jobs to fit the situations. Participant names changed, as did hair style and color, beards and goatees, and sometimes a bit of plastic surgery or touch-up Botox became necessary. Some folks had to gain weight, others tried (seldom successfully) to lose weight. Requests for bariatric surgery or gender-reassignment surgery fell into the "pending" basket at the Bureau's headquarters.

Kip and Marty adopted superficial changes, ordered by the FBI. They did not list themselves as FBI agents or employees, but rather as independent contract workers under the guise of Good Security Services, LLC. Kip kept his thick salt and pepper beard short to go with a one-inch buzz cut over watery brown eyes. Marty morphed her gorgeous long, straight black hair into white blond with black roots, a stunning thirty-four-year-old ex-cop turned PI, turned FBI. Reg approved.

On this particular evening, several weeks later, they mingled in the airport lounge on a surveillance job to monitor and observe members of their WPP flock. They could pass for a sybaritic, fortyish light-skinned African-American guy accompanied by his heavily tanned, beautiful young Latina "niece" or "fiancé"—a mutual disguise which they liked.

Kip stared openly at her breasts. "The police shrink said I have chronic, sub-clinical depression. Bullshit. I'm just a lost soul."

Marty said, "Check out Rocco and Teri. What a pair." She peered through the window. "They are leaving now."

Once outside, Kip dashed as fast he could, chased the couple from their hotel along the road in front of the airline gates. He gained on them, then lost ground, then gained it back, next he fell over a suitcase, scraped his knee, then screamed in pain. "Stop. Stop. Stop. Question and answer time."

They still ran. Teri removed her spike heels, while Rocco raced to keep up with her. At last, out of breath, they stopped running and faced each other, breathless and red-faced.

Teri said, "All we did was fuck." She was still panting.

Rocco sweated profusely. "Babe, you were fabulous, even though you didn't get off. I did."

"Bastard. You men are all bastards." She huffed and puffed.

Kip said, "It's me, Crandall. You know…"

Rocco said, "Go away, asshole. Why follow us?"

"Cut the shit, you two. Marty, my partner, is in the airport lobby. Routine surveillance. Nothing fancy. Go inside."

They walked into the lobby, all hot and perspiring. Marty, hair and make-up still perfect, sat alone and calm in an isolated corner. "Well, well. Some Olympic runners, if I'm not mistaken."

Kip said, "We don't care what you guys do as long as you don't screw up the WPP. Sorry for the pun."

"What's a pun?" Terri asked.

"Never mind," Rocco said. "What do you want?" His breathing returned to normal as he wiped off the sweat with a handkerchief.

Marty said, "If Tony finds out, then he just might kill Teri or you, Rocco."

Kip said, "And if Maryanne finds out she might bolt. Either way, those are problems for us. Stop it. We don't like it. We don't want it. It fucks up all of us. Remember, nobody knows about the four of you. Nobody at the Landing or the goddamn nightclub. We don't want problems."

Rocco and Teri held hands. She said, "All we did was rent a room and fuck our brains out."

Kip said, "I'm so goddamn furious that…why in the hell ruin the whole deal? You two could get the mob after the others. Tony was a shooter. He's your fucking husband, Teri. A real wise guy. And that Dock would kick you guys out of there, if he knew." His eye twitched mercilessly.

Marty said, "Take it easy, Kip. They get the message. Everybody has to behave in the WPP to make it work."

Kip said, "And what the fuck, you two don't look the part either. Teri, you look like an eighteen-year-old blonde hooker in that black bodysuit. Rocco, in a white muscle shirt? You fuckbrain, you were a capo in the mob. Look respectable here."

Teri's gorgeous brown-tinted eyes narrowed to slits. "What about the two of you? A big-time, ugly Hawaiian shirt on you, Kip, and old pin-stripe slacks on her. That's not FBI. Fuck you." She gave them the finger. Rocco pulled her hand down.

Marty and Kip edged through a revolving airport door into the ink-black night filled with the roar of jets. She said, "Fuck them. This FBI stuff is so extreme and serious. We used to have more

27

fun. Work out at a sports club or have vodka and burgers and get drunk bowling or shoot pool. We didn't make much money or stay busy all the time, but it sure was fun. You always loved my earrings. Other parts, too."

Kip headed for their aging, unmarked, FBI sedan. He nodded. "You're right. Health insurance and disability insurance and dental insurance aren't much fun. Government is good to us. Let's finish our reports tonight. Tomorrow I meet with those assholes Tony and Rocco."

The next day, Kip slouched between Tony and Rocco on an ancient iron bench during their monthly meeting. Wooden slats were missing. This tiny city park, positioned between the shiny glass towers of downtown and the slimy slum of the southern section, carried a reputation for drugs and crime. An ideal place to meet.

Tony said, "I'm sick of all this shit. I can't do what I want. Teri and me don't have no life." His arm bumped Kip's shoulder.

Kip asked, "Rocco? Are you unhappy, too?"

He shook his head. "Not like him, but Maryanne wants to be an accountant, not a singer in a titty bar. She's smart. College and all that."

Kip said, "I'm only the messenger. You guys signed up for this. You're alive and free. Well, not in some stinky federal prison for twenty years. Think about it."

Tony shifted his bulky weight from side-to-side slowly. "Teri thinks we should take our chances. Go somewhere else. No more Feds."

"Come on, Tony, you know they'd find you in a heartbeat," Kip said. "Our program works." His fists clenched and the muscles in his arms tensed and bulged. He touched the scar, now thicker with deeper furrows.

"Maybe we should leave, too," Rocco said. "Volunteering at a fucking homeless joint. I'd make five or ten large in a truck heist at the big airports."

Kip said, "We take care of you."

Rocco said, "Yeah, but we feel like shit. Weak. Like a child." He pretended to wipe away tears. "Boo-hoo."

Kip knew what he meant. They were dependent, WPP calling the shots, setting the rules, and providing the basics. Just like poor countries often end up hating America when it gives money, loans, food and tells them how to be democratic like us.

"Guys, I think I understand. There's no perfect deal. The Bureau understands, too." Kip slowly removed a digital recorder from his briefcase. "Let's take a trip down memory lane. They had all your friends and enemies, even some lawyers, wired in the old days. Listen to this."

Tony: I, Claudio Grinaldi, plan to whack you, Mr. Broker, in ten seconds if you don't tell me where the diamonds are. Ten, nine…

Broker: Okay, okay. Don't get in such a hurry. They're in the velvet lining of the box in the back room.

Tony: Go get them. Now. Eight, seven…

Broker: Untie my hands so I can carry them more easily.

Tony: No. Six, five…

Broker: Here, take the whole lot. They'll fit into your big fist. You fat Polack bastard.

Tony: On second thought, I'll just beat the shit out of you with the butt of my gun. Four, three… (sound of bone crunched)

Broker: You smashed my jaw. My nose must be broken!

Tony: On third thought, here's a bullet in your brain from the boss. (Shot fired)

Tony struggled to his feet. He picked up a trash can and threw it wildly, the bottles, garbage, and used drug paraphernalia flying everywhere. "You threatening me, you fucking slob? I testified, didn't I?"

"How about it, Rocco?" Kip asked. "Here's another digital beauty, your dearly beloved and a Federal prosecutor chatting one afternoon."

Maryanne: I only did what the boss told me to do.

Federal lawyer: What did he tell you to do, Mrs. Martini?

Maryanne: Hide the money. Launder the money. Don't let us

look rich to Uncle Sam. You've got the damn tapes and files.
Federal Lawyer: You had an MBA in Finance and you were a CPA in NY State?
Maryanne: Yes, that's correct.
Federal Lawyer: Don't you have professional responsibility? Ethical responsibility to do the right thing? Behave within the law. Isn't that right, Mrs. Martini?
Maryanne: I did not intentionally break the law. I only followed the orders of my superiors—the head of our family. And I am a woman. What do you expect?
Federal Lawyer: You violated professional canons, betrayed your whole educational preparation, and several laws of NY State and the nation.
Maryanne: I did not, sir. I never intended or planned to break the law. Not once. Never.

Tony faced Kip. He punched the air with both fists. "This job might not be good for your health."

Rocco crossed himself and let out a banshee scream. "You fuckers! You double-crossing fuckers."

Kip grabbed Rocco by the throat and squeezed until Rocco gagged, his eyes bulging and very wide. Kip said, "I'll let my superiors know that you wish to continue in the program, but that it's not perfect." He dropped the recorder into his briefcase as he walked away.

Tony said, "Okay, asshole, say what you want. I miss everything and everyone."

Rocco rubbed his neck while he mumbled slowly, his face half-hidden in both hands, "Mr. FBI, if you ever do anything to Maryanne, I'll pop you. Count on it."

Kip's thick facial scar heated up even more and he knew the bright crimson could be seen under his beard. He couldn't stop the eye twitch. His heart raced while his breathing turned rapid with plenty of whispered blowing. He bit his tongue until he was alone.

"These goddamn ingrates. We save their asses after a life of crime, let them live a decent middle-class life as a volunteer, and they want to walk out. No judgment, no planning, no brains. Fuck them all. They wouldn't last a week on the streets. Shoot their collective mouths off, brag about the past, or flash some old, gold jewelry, then bang, bang, bang, bang, four dead victims of the crime families they'd ratted out. Whacked by the mob hand that fed them all those years, while biting the FBI hand that feeds them now. I'm calling Marty. I need a drink."

A few nights later, when the explosive emotions had cooled, Kip crowded the front bench seat of the Ford van, tucked in between Rocco and Tony. Like Dock, he also evaluated their volunteer efforts. The sandwiches, coffee and donut program, and then presented his data to the WPP superiors. He hoped that Rocco and Tony eventually could each have their own van, signifying their importance to the Landing.

Tony said, "I like Dock to ride along. Not you."

A distinctive voice from the dark rear of the van startled them. "Keep going, Rocco, but I've got a damn sharp steak knife pointed at your head."

Tony said, "Is that you, Squeaky? I'd know you anywhere."

"I want money. Fuck your shitty, stale food," Squeaky said. "I want a bus ticket."

"Why didn't you come to me? Ask for help?" Tony turned toward Squeaky.

Rocco said, "I'm going to pull over and stop, so we can talk. No tricks." He braked on the side of the road.

"Where's the cash?" Squeaky said. "I need money. I've got TB and I'm going to Denver to a special hospital."

Tony said, "They've got pills now for TB." He laughed and slapped his leg. "You dumb shit, you don't need no hospital."

"I don't want no pills. I want money. Give it."

Kip was stunned when Squeaky slid the side door open, jumped out, and stumbled through a rocky, overgrown field near an abandoned service station.

Tony pointed toward the door. "Fuck him."

Rocco nodded. "Yeah, fuck him. I'll turn off the engine."

Kip struggled out of the door and caught him easily. The pace was slow due to Squeaky's health and ripe old age of seventy-nine.

Squeaky huddled against an oil drum on the ground, shaking and breathless from the brief run. "I'm so goddamn scared."

Kip approached. "I know. I'll get you meds. We'll get to the hospital. Trust me." He cradled Squeaky's head and shoulders in his arms as he kneeled next to him.

"No police. No cops," Squeaky said. He coughed heavily, forcing up dark blood. He wheezed and spat repeatedly, then grabbed his side. "Helluva pain. I need help. Yessirree, I do. This is my life, my city. No hospital. Leave me on the streets."

Kip said, "I'll see to it. Hang on to me. We'll walk back to the van. You'll be out of the hospital in no time."

On the drive to the hospital, Kip said, "You two guys behave yourselves. Don't get into trouble." Certain that the warning was necessary, even though he didn't know the specifics of the trouble ahead.

Chapter Four

Kip collaborated with Bill, his new Sponsor in AA. He called him whenever he needed to talk, night or day. Bill listened, encouraged, wheedled, begged, blamed, advocated the Big Book, whatever it took. Sensing his own helplessness, Kip ceded control to his Higher Power, thereby gaining some measure of personal discipline and individual responsibility for his life.

After a meeting Bill said, "Volunteer. Gets you out of yourself. Start here, at the Landing. These homeless fucks sure need it."

Kip located a sign-up sheet requesting volunteers on a bulletin board near their AA meeting room. Since he'd been a cop, an army MP, and had a few college classes under his belt, he was a natural mentor for the Landing. Being half-black didn't hurt, either.

He spoke to the director of volunteer services as the next step. The answer came fast.

"I'll start you with a kid. Mentor the hell out of him. Name is Tottie. It won't be easy."

Kip met Tottie the next day in the parking lot turned basketball court. At ten, he was still in second grade. "Hi, I'm Kip." He dwarfed the skinny black kid.

Tottie missed a free throw. "So, what's up?"

"Well, they call me a mentor," Kip said. "I'd like to get to know you and be of help, if you'll let me."

Several junkies and drunks slept it off nearby wrapped in black plastic garbage bags.

A slight drizzle fell from the ominous, grey skies. Tottie pulled up his hoodie. "I can always use more money or food."

They scooted quickly into the covered courtyard to stay dry. Kip dribbled the ball and passed it to Tottie.

Kip said, "We'll go out for lunch or dinner next time. What's school like for you?"

"It sucks. I don't always go." He shot the ball so hard against the side of the building that it bounced into the rain. He didn't chase it. Kip did.

"What do you do instead?' Kip asked. He juggled the ball from hand-to-hand.

"Hang out on the streets, go to shelters, get free clothes and food and sleep." Tottie held out his upturned hands, expecting Kip to pass the ball.

Kip held the ball. "Sounds boring. How do you get money?"

Tottie gazed into Kip's narrowed eyes. He lowered the hoodie. "I do what I want. Are you black? You don't look it. Do some magic. I don't spell for shit. Reading sucks. Look what I've got." He flipped open a six-inch switchblade, dull black handle with a shiny, polished pointed blade.

"Can I see it?"

"Sure." Tottie pressed the button to close it with a loud click before he gave it to Kip.

He put it in his pocket. "No knives or guns or bombs here."

"Give it back," Tottie said. "Fuck you volunteers." He walked away, then turned his head back. "I'll just get a bigger one."

Kip said, "We'll have dinner soon."

Tottie said, "I got business now," as he popped the hoodie over his head and ran into the rain.

Kip's eye twitched. He wiped off the basketball and kicked it back onto the wet court.

As he walked into the building he shook the water from his jacket. It was easy to receive permission from the Landing's social worker to call Tottie's teacher. "Yes, he is often tardy, frequently in detention, with low grades and high absenteeism. Social promotion," she said. "There's one other thing. He's very creative. He drew a pastel of street life and was voted the best artist in his elementary school by the staff. Thanks for your interest, Mr. Kip."

Kip followed through on the teacher's comments. He bought Tottie art supplies, an easel, watercolors, oil paints, brushes, and so on. He set up the easel at their next session. "Hope you like this stuff, Tottie."

Tottie walked out. Kip ran after him in the hallway. "We'll go bowling or shoot pool, have some fun."

"Can't make no money painting. It sucks," Tottie said.

Kip called the teacher again. "I'm having difficulty relating to him."

She said, "No surprise. I've offered him an alternative school, or even a chance, a good one, to compete for admission to an art and drama magnet school. I'd be ashamed to repeat his answer. He's impossible."

Kip knew first-hand about walking a new path in life. How the hell do you accept something that's awful? He had a sponsor and a Higher Power to believe in. He'd find some way with Tottie.

Kip slept late the next morning, weary from the mentor's mixed bag. Heartbreaking decisions competing with hopeful plans. He'd meet his protégé again that afternoon for a hastily arranged early dinner. To prepare, he reviewed some background information and written reports supplied by the director of volunteers.

A recent social worker summary updated Kip: "The name typed on the kid's birth certificate identified him as Reginald L. Williams, III. At age eight, the nickname Tater Tot stuck to him. Now, at ten, he answered to Tottie. Once he learned to read big words, as he called them, he'd understand that he struggled onto this planet in a federal prison hospital, nearly choked to death by his own umbilical cord. If the obstetrics nurse hadn't taken an unusually short smoke break, he might not have made it.

"Mother, Lucinda Williams, unmarried at the time and serving ten years for prostitution and drug dealing, simply liked the name Reginald and the thought of him as the third, with Roman numeral III after his name, impressed her. Father, truly unknowable. Lucinda didn't care much anyway, since she had many other kids by different men being raised by her own mother, and they were all boys. She wanted a girl but no matter how many dates, who the tricks were, no John could father a daughter for her, at least not yet.

"So Tottie lived off and on the streets, in shelters, with foster families, and sporadically attended school. Now in second grade again, his two favorite parts of the school day were lunch and recess. Unless the weather was so cold or wet that recess took place inside the schoolroom or auditorium, not on the playground. Tottie, tall but skinny for a second grader, loved sports and excelled at basketball and baseball. He also enjoyed punching others and wanted boxing to be an accepted part of recess. Sometimes he smoked tiny cigars the size of cigarettes, and liked the taste of Cognac.

"When it suited him, he walked away from his grandmother's tiny, crowded home, or foster care, and ran with the homeys, as he called the homeless. He learned how to stay dry and safe, obtain slightly used clothes for free, eat one or two meals per day in a soup kitchen, or at the Landing, and nullify any kind of adult supervision or control. He acted as if he were in high school or college based on a self-designed curriculum of ghetto cred and street smarts. He even perfected skills as a pickpocket at his school."

In his mind, Kip "adopted" Tottie, along with big plans. Soon he would take him to the dentist for check-ups, to the community clinic if lice infested his scalp again, and to the school principal to pressure him to enroll Tottie in an alternative school for kids in homeless shelters or foster care.

They met for dinner at a local burger joint. Kip really liked the kid's energy and spunk, despite it all, and nurtured unrealistically high hopes. He bought him a burger, fries, and a chocolate shake. Gone in a flash.

"Can I have another?" Tottie asked.

Kip sipped his coffee. "Of course. Didn't you get a good hot lunch at school?"

Tottie smiled. "Not today."

Kip said, "Hey, you mean no school or no hot lunch? Which is it?" He took a small bite of his broiled chicken sandwich, losing the tomato slice in the process.

Tottie said, "Both."

"You're only ten. You act like you're nineteen. Get an education and you'll be ahead of the game." Kip walked to the counter and ordered Tottie the same thing again. He returned to the booth.

Tottie shook his head. "That's bull."

Kip grimaced. "And I had a bit of college." He drummed his fingers on the table.

"And you just help losers." He nearly choked as he sucked on a straw.

Kip shook his finger at Tottie. "I think it's important to help street kids like you. Real important. So you don't end up a loser."

"Oh, come on, old man. Just makes you feel like you're a some-body." He sat ramrod straight. "I want to be somebody, too."

"I'll pick up the burger and fries now. Catsup?"

"Extra pickles."

Kip sat down. "What about school?"

"I hate it." He took a huge bite of burger.

Kip's appetite withered. His face sagged in dismay. "Why not stay at your grandmother's?"

"I hate it. My older brothers beat me up." A handful of fries disappeared.

Kip shook his head, then sighed and twisted in his chair. "I've got my work cut out for me with you. What do you want?"

Tottie swallowed the last bite, pulled out the straw, and gulped the shake. He wiped his mouth awkwardly on his sleeve. "I want good tattoos of Jesus. I want to lead a good gang. I want good money so I can buy a gold Cadillac sedan and plenty of gold jew-elry. I want what I want." He wiggled his fingers. "Gold rings and bracelets and watches."

Kip said, "The word is that your mother is still in prison. She sells dope. Is that what you want for yourself?"

Tottie closed his big brown eyes for a moment. "Life ain't a rose bush."

"So, you want to sell dope on the street all your life and be the head honcho in a gang? End up in prison?"

Tottie, cool as a cucumber, did not visibly tremble or sweat, or otherwise appear uncomfortable during this "interrogation."

"Never even been in juvie." He winked at Kip. "Okay, I'll go back to school."

Kip knew he lied about school. He knew about Tottie's dope-selling and that he hid money somewhere. If he followed him he might find the hiding place. The kid was plenty savvy. What the hell, lots of young guys were uneducated in any formal sense, fleeing from screwed-up families, bolstered by lessons they learned on the street.

Kip said, "I'll try to find you a job, part-time in the late afternoon after school. I doubt if I can. It won't be easy at your age." He flirted with the idea of throwing the kid through the plate-glass window.

"I knew you'd help me. I don't care about the rules," Tottie said. "I can con people. I've got a sales job."

"I know. I hope you'll change. You must change. I want to trust you. I'm not sure how far to go with you." Kip touched the knife wound, recalling the searing pain of that incident.

Tottie said, "Trust me. I'll paint. I'm good at it." He ran out the door and did a cartwheel on the sidewalk in front of the restaurant's window.

That night Kip asked himself what volunteering at the Landing so he could mentor the homeless really meant to him. Was it worth it? Doubts about the task crept into his thinking, given the situation with Tottie and the impossibility of any responsible adult turning him loose to his mother's whims and crimes. Tottie would never live with her if she got out of prison. He'd simply run away and return to the streets.

Kip's mind drifted. At an earlier time, he tried hard to be a mentor to Larry, his younger brother. Larry didn't like school though Kip encouraged and supported him in trying to succeed there. Larry had plenty of ability, but not the drive or energy to engage himself seriously in learning and studying. Four years younger than Kip, he nonetheless sailed through elementary school. Once in high school, things blew up. The drug culture sucked him into its orbit. Kip came home on his first leave from army boot camp and found Larry stoned in the basement of the family home.

"What's going on?" Kip asked.

Larry giggled and inhaled a huge toke. He coughed and laughed and promptly passed out.

Kip let him sleep it off for several hours. "What's going on, brother? Just experimenting?" He put his arm around Larry, seated close to him on the couch.

Lids heavy, his fifteen-year-old body limp, Larry said, "No, I'm into booze and drugs. I like it. I feel so…"

Kip loosened his military shirt and tie, then arose from the old, brown leather couch with the familiar holes and cracks in the seat. "Sorry to hear it. Not a good way to go. You know that."

"Can't stop, big brother. Really into it. Especially bourbon and pot. Mom and Dad don't have any idea. I come down here and do my thing."

Kip said, "What about school? Going to finish high school?"

Larry said, "Hell no. I've got a part-time job at KFC. I get high and then I fry. It rhymes…" He circled his hand, a miniscule roach between index finger and thumb.

Kip grabbed Larry's shirt front and shook him hard, till his head jerked back and forth several times. "It's stupid. No good will come of it. You're wasting your smarts. At least go into the service like I did."

Larry hung himself in a prison cell at age sixteen, after a petty crime to get drug money. Despite such painful, frustrating memories, Kip pledged to himself that he would continue with the mentoring. He was not going to give up on the homeless or himself! He did his best for Larry, as did their parents.

Kip's exhaustion led to a long, dreamless sleep. After a hot shower and clean clothes, he wolfed down bacon and eggs and drank plenty of hot, black espresso. He felt fortified sufficiently to call the volunteer coordinator at the Landing. He was given a recommendation for two more men who needed plenty of mentoring, including educational, social service, and career.

Squeaky and Namey, regulars at the Landing, were well-known by other street people. He could see them without delay.

Looking professional in khakis and blue button-down shirt, Kip plopped his six-foot frame on the edge of a metal desk in a small, airless, interior office at the Landing. Two chairs in front of the desk held Squeaky and Namey, apparently groggy after a huge lunch of hot dogs, beans, cornbread, lemonade, and Twinkies.

"I'm Kip, a volunteer here." He attempted to shake hands with each of them.

Squeaky's handshake was weak and uninvolved. "Howdy. I remember you. Got me to the hospital," he said. "They call me Squeaky, 'cause of my voice. Took shrapnel in my neck and throat from them Cong." He stood, ready to leave the room, but Kip motioned him to sit again.

Namey did not shake hands. "Don't touch," he said. He averted his gaze toward the blank wall.

Squeaky said, "He lost his friends in Iraq. Don't talk much. Never uses his real name. Was a sergeant."

Kip said, "How can I be of help to you guys? We need a plan. I'm in AA so I know the agony of trying to beat problems."

"That's not me. Nope. I'm not a big drinker," Squeaky said. "Some wine now and then with street people. That's it."

Namey closed his eyes.

Kip asked, "Well, Squeaky, what do you need?"

"Vietnam was the best part of my life. I'm almost eighty years old and I've got TB and HIV. I want to go to Colorado to get rid of them diseases. That's it. The fucking VA has fucked me over. I get a little disability but the VA Hospital is a shit hole." He re-lit a damp, cheap cigar and blew out a storm. His bony hand covered with parchment-like skin lazily swiped the smoke upward. He stomped on the cigar butt.

Kip slid off the desk and stood close to Squeaky. "You're fed up with the VA. You need medical services. You want to move to Colorado."

"You got it, bud. Combat engineers like me only get to be laborers. I can't even do that shit now," Squeaky said. Then he bent over and coughed up blood mixed with sputum and vomit onto the table. He wiped it up with his shirt sleeve and tattered sweater. "Sorry, sir. That damn TB acts up."

"I'll try to arrange medical help. I'll tell the volunteer director right away," Kip said.

"I'm a goner." He coughed again, gagging on his own mucus.

Kip said, "It could help. They can cure TB."

"I'm not con, con, contagious anymore. Some nurse promised me." He rolled tobacco into cheap, yellow, cigarette paper, lit it with a wooden match, and puffed a huge cloud of acrid smoke. "There now, that's better."

Namey, blank eyes in a frozen face, turned to look impassively at Squeaky. He said, "Nothing matters."

Kip couldn't gauge Namey's age, guessed he might be around forty. "Namey, is there anything you need?"

"More meds," Namey said. "More meds."

Kip said, "They told me you were a good mechanic."

Namey avoided eye contact and remained silent, presenting an immobile, robotic face. It reminded Kip of zombies, with no affect, yet always ready for a good meal of human blood and flesh.

Kip opened a small case. "Take a look at these." He held up a black and white drawing. "They gave me some pictures to show you. Different feelings or emotions on each face. Good practice to say what you think each face says."

Namey said, "Screw it. No trust."

"Why not?" Kip asked.

"Just don't."

"Maybe, just maybe, I can find a way to help you, even if there's no trust." He held out his right hand.

Namey didn't answer. He pushed several fingers through his stringy hair, showing Kip his lower arm, visibly decorated with old tracks and new grime. "Squeaky helps." Arms now at his sides, he stood, looked straight ahead, did an about face, and quickly marched out.

Squeaky followed. "Hey, wait up, Namey."

Kip updated the volunteer coordinator, and suggested medical service for both men. He then called Bill and told him about Tottie, Namey, and Squeaky.

Bill said, "Stick with it. Help you stay sober. Even doctors and social workers fuck up."

That night Kip rejected several possibilities; beat his head against a wall, throw a bowling ball through a church window, or hit some innocent cat or dog with his car. He reminded himself of his curiosity about the homeless and his need to keep trying to relate and serve. He felt divided between cop and caretaker, with the empathy and understanding of the latter taking over for the time being.

A week later. He planned to talk to other volunteers. He read a self-help book on how to help others. The evening he finished the book, Kip took a call on his cell as he walked to his car.

"I'm Tottie's mother. I'm on probation in a local half-way house. Jail was so crowded they let me out. I need to see you, Mr. Mentor. And soon."

"That's fine. I'd be glad to talk with you about Tottie's welfare."

"He ain't no welfare case. That's me," she said.

"How about noon tomorrow? We can talk and have lunch at the Landing." He muffled a belch.

"No way, José," she said. "Make it that burger joint down the street from you."

"Okay. What do I call you?" He opened the car door.

"Oh, Mrs. Williams will be just fine. Don't rightly know where Mr. Williams is though."

"Call me Kip. I'll be in a booth by the window. See you there, Mrs. Williams." He sat in the driver's seat and folded his arms. Laugh or cry, he couldn't decide which, probably both. Out of the frying pan into the fire.

Kip fantasized as he adjusted the seat belt, an ex-cop turned PI turned mentor having lunch with a black crack-head, ex-con, probably a whore, at a burger joint to discuss her son, if he was her son. He answered himself, "I'm a volunteer at a homeless center who's trying to mentor a wild, young black kid who's lived on the street most of his life." It still didn't sit very well with him.

Kip took the same booth at the window he'd shared with Tottie. He ordered coffee and waited for her. And waited. And waited. Precisely at 12:45 p.m., he presumed it was Mrs. Williams who strutted into the restaurant, dressed in an ankle-length purple and white print dress, black patent-leather spike heels, and a wide-brimmed purple hat adorned with long, white feathers. She spotted him immediately.

"Sorry I'm late but the Reverend Dr. Washington kept me after choir practice," she said. She fluttered her eyelids as she took her seat.

She'd probably been a looker at some point, but hard street life took its toll, leaving a scarred, pimply face, largely hidden under too much make-up, blood-shot narrow eyes and hands with knobby joints.

She held out both hands with palms down. "What do you think of long, fake nails, a cross on each of them?"

Kip ignored the question. "What will you have?" he asked. He took his hands off of the table and played with the paper napkin.

"Whatever you're having," she said. "Heard that line at a prison movie night."

"I'm having coffee and a large burrito with the works." He slid to the end of the bench seat.

"Okay by me. By the way, I need money real bad." She polished her two gold front teeth with a finger.

Kip went to the counter to order the food. He picked it up and sat down with the tray.

She said, "I need money now," then took a huge bite.

"I'm here to talk about Tottie. I'm called his mentor, his helper."

"I know that. I need money. Get me some. I'll do anything. Drugs, sex, steal, whatever it takes. I'm a survivor." She adjusted her neckline.

"What about Tottie?" That familiar twitch in his left eye fired up.

"Look, Mr. Mentor, I need money. I got a bunch of kids live all over. Social workers calls my 'issue.' Tottie's a street kid. He'll make it." She hungrily wrapped her leg around one of his.

"Well, Mrs. Williams, how's your burrito?" He pulled away on his side of the booth.

"Tastes like shit. I need a drink."

Kip's feet shook. He drummed his fingers on the table. His eye twitched faster. His breathing became more rapid. Then pain in the middle of his chest. Try to relax he told himself, it's only heartburn. He took out an antacid pill and crushed it, choked it down with his coffee.

"Tottie's a good kid, you know," Kip said. "Some behavior problems, but he's very young. He'll work it out. Not everybody goes to Harvard. Nor do they…"

"Fuck that shit. He's a conniving little crook. You can't trust him. He's a bullshitter of the first order. Steal your shoes right off your feet." She swallowed her burrito in one more bite. "That little so-and-so sent me a Mother's Day card one year. Don't know for the life of me how he got my address at the prison. Must have stole the card. I should have given him something at Christmas, but shit, I didn't have a goddamn penny. Not one red cent."

Kip said, "Anyway, he doesn't go to school very often. Hates it at his grandmother's, says his older brothers beat him up. He sleeps on the street or at the Landing most of the time." He thought of grabbing this woman and dumping her out on the sidewalk. No way, José. No way he'd be sent to prison for this bitch. When she pulled a cigarette out of her purse, he noticed a tiny, pearl-handled .22 pistol.

Mrs. Williams gulped half her coffee with three creams and four sugars. "He's a lying motherfucker. There ain't no grandma, he ain't got a brother living in the state, and he ain't seen me for a couple of years. He's a lying little fuck that deserves what he gets. I hope to Christ he is my last. I nearly died having him."

She chugged down the rest of her coffee and, without asking, wrapped Kip's half-eaten burrito in a napkin. "I'll give it to one of the wetbacks where I live. Don't forget, I need money real bad."

Kip felt shot-down by his low success rate. He could connect Squeaky with medical services, but Namey held him at bay. Tottie was a crazy, wild kid, a product of the streets, a liar but strangely honest. Fortunately, mentoring at the Landing deepened his interest in homeless people and their plight. So many stories, from street kids to two vets from different wars.

Maybe he'd be more gratified from his further contract work with the Police FBI Task Force. The professional part of his career with Marty blossomed at the Bureau, after they investigated the Salvation Army and St. Francis. Reg liked their unassuming approach. Kip longed for the chance to get a better view of Dock and his shenanigans at the Landing.

Chapter Five

The next afternoon in the director's office, Dock, Tony, and Rocco negotiated.

Dock said, "We're going to cook up a good scheme. How do we divide the pie?" He stroked his smooth-shaven face on both cheeks. Then he did a full 360-degree swivel in his desk chair. "How will we split up the dough?"

Tony said, "Look, Mr. Director, you called this meeting. How do we do the green stuff?" Both apron and shirt were grimy, his watery brown eyes hiding excitement and greed.

Rocco rearranged his chair to point directly at Dock. He rolled up the sleeves of his newly starched black shirt and tweaked his gold necklace. "You did say it involved pot, didn't you? What the fuck. Let's put our cards on the table."

"Hold it, you two big shots. Don't get ahead of yourselves," Dock said. "Are you in or out? That's the final question. Yes or no?"

Tony said, "Dock, all you said you knew some kind of a fucking way to make a lot of bread with pot. In or out of what?"

Rocco said, "Tony's got a point. What the fuck?"

Dock walked to the office door, twisted the handle, then turned the bolt. "This is confidential." He opened it again, peeked both ways to make sure no one was in the hallway, and then locked it. "It's really very simple and there's absolutely no risk of getting caught. My contact grows it in Mexico, then we employ Mexican immigrants and homeless citizens, first as mules, then have them distribute and sell, street dealers."

"Shit," Tony said. "Those assholes would fuck us up in a second."

Dock pursed his lips and grimaced so hard his face nearly cracked in half. "If any employee of ours says a thing to cops or anyone else, they are dead. That's it. Any deviation, they not only don't get paid, they get dead."

Rocco nodded. "No witnesses."

Tony said, "These fucking panhandlers. Always another one to take their place."

"And don't forget," Dock said, "that the cops usually ignore dead immigrants with no papers. Adios. Bye-bye to those we have to kill." He waved his right hand slowly.

Tony said, "Boss, get down to brass tacks. How's it work? If it ain't good, forget about it."

"Here's the whole enchilada. Either our mules or the cartel people bring it to the Landing's storage areas. We repackage it and ship it out across the country. Homeless guys, the street dealers, make money selling it. They travel a lot so nobody notices them. They've got a good cover. We'll put a few kids with them to make it look legit."

"How much?" Rocco said. His hands quivered with excitement.

"Plenty. Hundreds of kilos a year. We ought to clear about a million a year to start, after expenses. I'll divert the $50,000 from our federal-government grant to help the homeless to pay for the initial buy-in. How's that?"

Tony said, "Not bad. Maybe that's why you're a doctor. I'm in." They shook hands.

"Me too," Rocco said. "Definitely." First a thumbs up, then a handshake.

"Here's what you two do. Tony, you run the storage area. Rocco, you run the distribution. I take fifty percent and you each get twenty-five percent."

Tony struggled out of his chair. "Come on, Rocco, this is bullshit. We're not suckers."

Tony and Rocco walked to the door, fumbled with the deadbolt lock and hanging their heads, entered the hallway.

Dock overheard Tony say, "We should whack…"

Dock yanked the door open. "Come back, you two, get back in here."

Tony and Rocco slowly padded back into the office. They stood in front of the desk. Tony said, "Now what?"

"That was my opening salvo. That's what happens in fair-minded discussions among partners. Then there's haggling, back and forth. How about a drink?" He poured rye and water for them.

Rocco said, "We want equal shares. We've got wives. You came on like a greedy goombah, a real wiseguy. We've seen plenty of that shit." He sipped his drink, gaze on Dock.

Tony walked around the desk and towered over the seated Dock. "If you fuck us, we'll fuck you. Tell everybody what a scam artist you really are. You'll be in a prison cell."

Dock sweated and struggled to keep his mind clear. "That's no way to talk to a partner. Tit for tat. I could snitch about both of you and the pot scheme. You'd be in a cell, too. Maybe worse, depending on what you've done before."

Rocco laughed. "Guess we're even, boss. How about thirty-thirty-forty? Think about it." They walked out.

Dock didn't have a moment to think. He received an urgent phone call reporting that Buster had gone wild in his enclave. He toppled tents, crashed bottles, lit a small grass fire, screamed, yelled and cursed and otherwise raised so much hell that his buddies called the cops. They dumped him in the drunk tank. He cried and sobbed and puked all over the aluminum bench, bolted to the jail wall.

The desk sergeant blared into his cell phone, "We've got him, Dock! Your boy Buster. The wine got him good this time. His nose is real red and it bleeds some."

"I'll be right over and take him to detox at the hospital."

Dock stored "work" clothes in his office closet. He pulled on jeans and an old brown hoodie with the word "Home" barely visible on the front. He ran through the hallway and out to the public parking lot, now filled end-to-end with sleeping bags and blankets rolled up like huge tacos filled with the homeless. He stopped short, then charged out to the back of the center where the few paid staff could park.

He drove to the jail and found Buster's holding cell. "I've got chocolate bars in the car, Buster. We're off to detox."

Buster snored.

Dock said, "I'll be damned if I'll spend good taxpayer money to have EMTs cart you to detox. Get off your ass." He shook him hard, hands on his shoulders, but to no avail.

"Guard, could I kindly have a blanket? Please call me after he sleeps it off and cleans up his mess."

The guard found a thin brown blanket for Dock. He wrapped Buster in it, then saluted him as he left the tank. "You drunk son of a bitch." Dock smothered his nose with a handkerchief to ward off the stench.

On the ride back to the center, Dock ruminated. Detox works for a few days, rehab for a few weeks, and AA for months or years if one makes a daily commitment to a higher power, attends meetings religiously, and uses a sponsor. Buster fell through the cracks. For him, nothing worked very well for very long. Cheap red wine overwhelmed, literally conquered him, every prevention effort and treatment that had been tried, including hospitals, medication, detention in jail, a work-farm program, and behavioral therapy. Buster lived the life of a chronically homeless alcoholic. A human, societal and medical black eye, and to no one's surprise, so had his father. Both parents had burned to death when a fire consumed the abandoned, boarded-up house where they slept.

Dock worked the center's halls later that night. After he finished off a bologna sandwich and lentil soup in the kitchen, he met Karen in the common area. "How do you do, I'm Dock."

"Nice to meet you, I'm Karen."

He admired two things about her right away. She sat upright in the club chair, back straight, long dark hair and head tilted very slightly, giving her an inquisitive but proud appearance. She smelled so good, her sweet perfume reminiscent of what he'd known as a child growing up with his mother and sisters.

Dock surprised himself when he impulsively opened up to her, like sharing with his sisters. He said, "I wanted to be a jet fighter pilot. Climbing and action defined me. Trees, roller coasters, sports, jumping off the high dive at the swimming pool, gangs, and especially driving fast and recklessly. We moved a lot since my dad was a salesman. It was so boring at home, so ordinary, so middle-class. Then there was the thrill of what I did later on. You won't believe me...sort of a bad boy. I learned a lot about how to beat the system at its own game."

Karen said, "That's an interesting story. My two girls have suffered plenty. I'm just hanging on, not quite ready to reveal myself or have a real committed relationship with anyone. My husband is still my husband, the abusive SOB, drinking and into drugs, while I don't have such clean hands either, so to speak. I drank too much. Divorce and counseling are ahead for us. And a job and good schools for my girls." She gathered herself, picked up her purse, ready to walk away.

Dock said, "How about a part-time job here at the Landing while we see what develops?" He came on to her fast, unglued by the aroma and her looks.

"That sounds great. Thanks. No promises, however. I can't forget." Her head drooped with lost pride. "Terrible nightmares and then it happens all over again. Some days I'm so afraid, I can't do much. See you later."

Dock flew down memory lane. Though it must have been more than three decades ago as Rod Mulligan, later Dr. Ralph Meade, now simply Dock, he remembered girlfriends and the family vividly. He rushed things, always in a hurry. He couldn't find the right woman, then or now. Had to be either quickie affairs or the blind trust of sisters and Mother. His Dad was the original bad boy.

Janelle, his oldest sister, said, "We know, too, but now Dad just drinks a lot."

The younger sister, Gayla, said, "The other women…he shouldn't have done it. Does Mom know?"

Rod said, "Who knows if she knows? I try not to think about it. Women and booze. I just have to think that Dad is a lost soul, doesn't know how to behave in a house run by women." He hugged both of them.

"You see a divorce coming soon? Isn't that right, Rod, a shitty divorce?" said Janelle. "He'll lie through his teeth. Mom had one affair. Who could blame her? He had so many. He'll screw her with the lawyers and the money."

Rod said, "You guys protected me from him and backed me up."

Gayle said, "So did Mom."

"I had a lot to hide," Rod said.

49

Chapter Six

The Dallas DA agreed with the FBI decision for Kip and Marty to impersonate homeless clients, obtain services at the Landing, and become personally acquainted with Dock. Rumors were flying about the center. The DA knew that it would be impossible to use undercover Dallas cops, since they would be easily recognized by so many homeless shelter inhabitants.

Kip explained to Rocco and Tony that he and Marty would be at the Landing, disguised in homeless garb, as part of an on-going investigation. He said, "You two hoods keep your mouths shut about us; be sure to follow the lead of your new babysitter." He'd tell Tottie, Squeaky, and Namey that he was now a street person. Lost his job and homeless.

Kip and Marty quickly wrapped up their WPP jobs. They drove near downtown on the final Friday night in a nondescript blue sedan, e-mailing their final updates on fifteen people to a phony account. Their hard drives were destroyed monthly once they were assigned new ones. Marty requested one of the new "tablets" but had been added to a waiting list.

The Bureau behaved cautiously with these teams, just as it did with those in hiding. Kip often felt in as much limbo as the ex-witnesses, quite vulnerable, and nearly as deceitful. Who the hell could one trust in this world? On the other hand, the money had been pretty good and steady.

Kip and Marty willingly took on the new assignment, but remained ambivalent, unconvinced that this undercover operation by ex-PIs made any sense. They had their work cut out for them with a number of daunting questions and issues. Had the FBI and other agencies done their best? Did the Dallas police, even the DA, perform their jobs with competent, patient investigations? Were some contacts in Dallas dangerous to individuals in witness protection? What about the Landing? And Dock, what of his background? Were the earlier rumors true? They'd been told that he partied with several of his volunteers, referred to them as his "clones," his "favorite mob," and wanted more of them.

Dock, Kip, and Marty met in his office.

"It could be just rumors, then again, who knows," Kip said. "We'll be undercover here. Among your staff or clients, a few guys know me. I used to volunteer here. They will be told that I'm now jobless and homeless."

Marty wore white leggings, three heavy sweaters, old Army boots, but no makeup. Even so, she looked damn good. "We'll just try to blend in and ask a few questions," she said.

Dock nodded, eyes narrowed. "It's a first. Undercover agents here. I can't imagine anyone in the Landing would be involved with felonies or major crimes or conspiracies. Doesn't involve us."

Kip's eye twitched. He scratched his face where the long neck-to-cheek knife wound scar heated up. "You just never know, Dr. Meade, or Dock, whichever you prefer. People talk, rumors grow. You never know."

"We'll help out, naturally. Just let me know what you need," Dock said. "Mr. Grund, the chairman of my Board of Directors, insisted that I cooperate."

"Mostly," Marty said, "so nobody suspects we're anything other than a homeless couple, a light-skinned black mutt and his brown woman. We're diversity on wheels. We drink a lot of vodka when we have money or red wine when we're broke. We both go to AA. We love rice and refried beans, and also boiled greens, hocks, and sweet potato pie." She bent over and retied the Army boot laces.

Kip said, "Several folks suggested that you, Tony, and Rocco are buddies—'The Three Musketeers' was the term."

Dock fingered the pen and pad on his desk. "We occasionally have a drink, usually rye and water, here in my office, but I've done that with others." He stood and walked around his desk so he could shake hands perfunctorily with each of them. "Count me in. Anything you need. Don't want cops unless we call 911 with a problem."

Kip said, "Looks kosher to me. Probably a dead end here." He tried to break the tension. "Can we have clean sheets?"

Kip and Marty explored the Landing. They embedded themselves in the vagaries of homeless life, where rainy days sent soaked bodies rushing into the center, wet clothes clinging to them, failed by their ancient, broken umbrellas. These unwashed folks, layers of clothing now drenched by rainwater, usually crowded into the dayroom. Slippery puddles on the floor and damp lounge chairs increased the unpleasant odor of human sweat and dirt, worsened by the rain rather than diminished. The humid dayroom, TVs blaring, stunk to high heaven as temperatures bumped ninety degrees.

Kip saw Marty cry as they observed an elderly woman straddle her walker, wet from head-to-toe, still suffering every drop of the downpour. No one gave her a chair though she stood dripping, hunched over in a corner. So much rain and so many tears, and so much pain.

Kip studied the cavernous lunchroom. It was a simple affair, steam tables along the wall near the kitchen, dirty, gray, linoleum-tile floor, pock-marked beige walls, and a flock of small tables with four chairs each. No murals, no art, no color. Crowding encouraged many to eat while standing or seated on the floor, backs against the wall. A cocktail party of sorts.

Kip said, "We'll stay together. You talk to the ladies and I'll take the guys."

"Sounds good to me."

They sidled up to an individual eating alone at a lunch table. "Want company? Soup is always too hot," said Marty.

"Sure, sit down…both of you. I'm Queenie. Folks generally stay away from me. Take a load off, or shoot your load, whatever fits. Before all this I danced at a club with a bunch of other trannies. No surgery for me, just pretend. A guy fucked and sucked me, two for the price of one. Not everybody, you know, just guys that were clean, real clean. I was so popular that the owner threw me out, said I stole all the business from the other girls. So I'm in transition, sort of biding my time on the street." She delicately blew on a spoonful of soup. "It's perfect now."

"I'm very, very clean but very, very much a lesbian, so we can just talk, if that's okay," Marty said.

Kip couldn't help eyeing Queenie's low-cut black tank top above expensive, skin-tight black jeans. Where did the money come from?

Marty said, "What's with this place? It's my first time. I lost my job as a meter maid when a few pennies accidentally rolled into my purse." All three of them chuckled.

"It's pretty nice. I sleep here a few times a week and try to eat at least once a day here. It's pretty nice. Good showers sometimes. All the old winos and druggies get a hard-on around me. They don't do that for just anyone." She shrugged, then rolled her shoulders and undulated her hips—full of grace and pride.

Marty said, "Anything unusual go on here? I wouldn't mind making a few bucks. Selling anything. Hear anything?"

"Now listen, I'm not a snitch. Fuck off, bitch. Are you both cops?" She wet her pink lips and raised her eyebrows over large hazel eyes.

"Sure, don't we look like it?" Marty said. "I'm just making conversation. I need a few bucks, that's all." She hadn't touched her soup. "I can't stand this shit." She spit in it.

"Well, there is something," Queenie said. "Plenty of rumors. Tony and Rocco get it on with Dock. You know, sexcapades after dark in his office. Booze. Sure wish I had been there. Must have been fun."

"Anything else you've heard or seen?" Kip asked. He couldn't stay out of the conversation for very long.

"One other thing, but I don't know for sure. About selling drugs. A young homeless guy, says he was a computer worker, told me one night in our tent that he planned to make thousands soon by traveling around and selling for the three of them, Rocco, Tony, and Dock. We'd had sex for several hours, so this cat was stoned and very relaxed and he might have been bullshitting or just bragging. Otherwise, he wasn't much to brag about, if you take my meaning." She blinked seductively.

Marty said, "Yes, I do." She grinned. "It is what it is. Maybe I could make a few bucks doing the same thing."

Now Queenie stood, raised herself to her full height, and looked down at Marty. "Do you mean sell drugs or have trannie sex with men in a tent?"

"The drug possibility."

After they interviewed Queenie, Kip and Marty meandered through the hallway to the outside plaza. The constant noise, the pungent odors, the terrifying screams, and the confusion of the Landing overwhelmed Kip. His mind returned to Iraq, to a dusty, mud-baked orphanage his unit stumbled into, ready to protect all of the children, shoot their way in and shoot their way out if they had to, then carry the kids to safety. They discovered the unthinkable. The kids' heads filled a huge mud vase at the rear of the main living area. No kids alive.

Kip struggled back to the present fast. Though hot with no wind, the coal-pellets blazing in an old oil barrel still attracted both him and Marty, and his former mentee, Namey. Each of them rubbed their hands vigorously over the flames.

Namey smoked something in a pipe. Kip respected the fact that he called himself Namey, joking that it was short for Nameless. He wore tattered army fatigues and a watch-cap pulled down to his eyes. "It's you, the volunteer?"

Kip said, "Yes. This is my friend Marty. Somebody mentioned that you did some stuff for the director. We're both here now. I'm not a volunteer. I'm homeless, too. I need money. Real bad."

Namey moved back from the barrel, dumped his pipe, and turned to walk away. "See you."

"Don't let me scare you away. I'm just trying to hustle a few bucks. Been laid off. Been rough. My ex-wife says my kid needs a dentist." Kip stroked his beard with filthy hands.

Namey stopped. "You cops?"

"Not at all. I've got my own problems," Kip said.

"See Dock."

"Is that it?" Kip kicked the barrel to re-start the flames.

"That's it." He jiggled the pipe-stem between his teeth.

"Thanks. I won't forget it. I owe you."

Namey looked Kip over from head to toe. "I like that coat."

Kip took it off and held up the shoulders of the coat so Namey could slip his arms into it. "Perfect fit, sir. Anything else?"

Namey said, "Go to the doctor with me after breakfast. Squeaky is sick now."

"Fine, I'll go. What should I do? What should I say? You know, how should I behave? Give me a clue, Namey."

Namey shrugged and pulled the army coat tighter around his chest. He pressed his index finger to his stained lips.

"I guess that means moral support only," Kip said. "Keep quiet."

Namey kept his finger on his lips as he walked away.

Kip and Marty remained next to the barrel fire for what seemed like hours. He felt painfully alone, both parents and his brother long dead. Wife lost to cancer. No other family he considered close or intimate. "I guess I have survivor's guilt," he said to Marty. "Why me? Could I have saved my brother? Or Wendy? I'm a lost soul left behind alive." He closed his eyes, irritated by the smoke, and held his head in his hands, weeping. He wanted some rest in his warm sleeping bag, better off than Namey in his used cardboard haven lined with old sweaters.

Marty simply held him, wrapping her arms around him as tightly as she could.

At coffee the next morning, Namey still wore Kip's coat. He waited in line for the VA outpatient clinic to open at 7:00 a.m. while Kip rode shotgun.

Once seated in the waiting room, Namey said, "I love movies. I'm undead."

A doctor yelled, "Robert Allen Wilson! Sgt. Wilson, please come to my office or you'll miss your appointment." Dr. Levin, nametag visible, now stood in front of him. "Come on, Bob. Your turn. It's okay."

The tiny, bald man with a flowing white beard led the way. Kip walked with them.

"Don't touch me," Namey said.

They followed Dr. Levin to the first cubicle, totally devoid of the usual insignia of a shrink. No diploma on the walls, no couch, no paintings, no sculpture, even no windows. Two straight-backed chairs stood in front of a tiny desk, with a double-locked headbanger medicine cabinet hugging the wall above it. Kip stood by the wall.

Dr. Levin's armchair held a donut cushion. He squirmed. "How goes the battle, Sarge?"

"I feel like shit," Namey said.

"Can we use your given name today?" He twirled his white beard into ringlets.

"I'm Namey."

Dr. Levin said, "Fine, for now it's Namey. Take your meds?"

"I forgot," Namey said. "I sold most for wine and four packs of Camels without filters." His hands shook and the sweat dripped down his face and neck.

Dr. Levin stood, then repositioned himself in his chair. "What the fuck do I do with you?"

Namey grinned. "I'm tri-polar. Up, down, sideways." He arose and stood at attention, saluted, and then held his arms rigidly at his sides.

Dr. Levin saluted. "If I give you pills, you sell them or trade for stuff that will kill you. If I don't, you suffer. We both lose both ways. Double-whammy. Stand at ease, trooper."

Namey slipped his arms behind him. "There's the shot?"

"Oh, Christ, you wouldn't let anybody close enough for that." Dr. Levin shook his head and closed his eyes.

"I'll die," Namey said.

"Before you do, take these." Dr. Levin handed him a small bottle of pills. "There's a week's worth. Then come back. Take them, one a day. You'll be less depressed. Go to the AA or NA meetings. Give it up to a higher power. It wasn't your fault that your platoon was killed."

Namey came to attention, saluted again, did an about face, and walked out. Kip followed. Without speaking, they left the clinic.

Kip returned to the Landing at 8:00 a.m., as the sun finally peeped through cloudy gray skies driven by a gusty wind. He saw Marty roll over in her sleeping bag in the outdoor plaza where men, women, and children slept catch-as-catch can, anywhere they could find a place. Breakfast line-up started at 6:30 a.m. and was nearly finished! She rolled out, tied up her bag, and stretched, before moving to the back of the line. Toilet time could wait, since the need for coffee and donuts took priority.

"God, it's so hot," Marty said. She blew on the coffee cup. "Where were you?"

Kip smiled. "You don't want to know. Believe me. They've got chocolate-covered donuts today. We didn't find out much last night."

"Not much, some hints about selling drugs, traveling to other cities. They're all scared shitless of getting involved." She dunked a donut and licked the hot icing.

Kip said, "I don't blame them. Probably got plenty to hide. We'll have to take a look in Dock's office. Maybe there will be a clue."

Kip felt a tug on his backpack, like a large-mouth bass swallowing a plug, strong but not the bite of ferocious bonefish. The young kid behind him, he knew it was Tottie, grabbed his backpack and ran across the plaza toward one of the wide doors that led to the alley behind the center.

He threw his baseball hat to the ground as he ran, then vaulted over a couple sleeping late in a double-wide bag. Kip chased him as fast as he could, but gained no ground. "Stop Tottie, that's my stuff! Give it back."

The kid raced ahead, energized by an apparently new pair of white running shoes. Kip wore boots and the kid was a fourth of his age.

"Hold up, you little bastard. I want my stuff. It's Kip. I'm homeless now. I'll let you go."

Tottie raced down the alley and turned into the boulevard at the side of the center. He either disappeared into one of the nearby buildings or else got picked up by the car of an accomplice. No Tottie in sight!

Kip jogged slowly back to Marty. She smiled as he huffed and puffed. "Not getting any younger, are you, big boy? You're still my guy, for better or worse." She rose on tip-toes and kissed him on the forehead.

Kip said, "I think I would have beaten the shit out of him if I caught him. I'm still a cop at heart. He's lucky I'm middle-aged and slowed down. The little bastard got the backpack but not much in it. That's my thanks for trying to mentor him."

Marty said, "Not much gratitude or love in this place. It's a pretty shitty life. What really goes on? Plenty of rumors about our boy Dock. What the hell are we going to find out?"

Kip wiped away the perspiration from his red face. "It's a scary place. You feel so vulnerable. Always on guard."

Chapter Seven

Years ago, Dock mourned his sisters, alone. Father already dead, his mother Eloise Mulligan lived in St. Louis, divorced but never remarried. Gifts sent to her by him on holidays or birthdays traveled by circuitous routes. He cooked up excuses to avoid mailing them from Dallas. Sometimes he went to the airport with small packages and paid travelers to mail them from their destinations. It worked. She knew he lived.

He decided to visit her. Dock still feared being caught and returned to prison as a parole violator, so he disguised himself for the trip to St. Louis. Driving to a distant section of Dallas, he visited a costume shop located in a nondescript, suburban strip mall. One side of the store sold masks and costumes, while the opposite wall held all manners of sex toys.

"How much is that wig" said Dock.

A guy in his mid-twenties, dressed Goth in all black, slipped on a Ronald Reagan mask and said, "Well, sir, that particular toupee, we call it the Samuel L. Jackson model is $200 on sale. He's the African-American movie star."

Dock said, "I know who he is. You think I live under a rock?"

"No sir, no offense, sir." His neck flushed.

The clerk now changed to a Superman mask. Next he wore a Spiderman neck and full-head covering. He must have plenty to hide, too.

"Do you have a matching goatee and mustache?" Dock lifted the wig to his head. He glanced in a mirror on the counter.

"Please don't do that unless you're going to buy it," the clerk said. He turned beet red.

"I'll give you $150 for it and another fifty dollars for the goatee and mustache." Dock liked the disguise, proud of his ability to haggle.

"That will be fine, sir. Halloween and Christmas are a ways off, so business is slow right now."

Dock located light green sunglasses at an optometrist's, then an intricately carved dark wood cane to help with his limp. A light wool grey-striped suit, a knock-off of Brooks Brothers, completed his outfit. Distinguished. Well-to-do. Cultured. He appeared to be a museum official, perhaps the head of a government division studying African culture, or the fund-raiser for a symphony. If Mom could be fooled, he could deceive anyone looking for him.

Although long-time parole violators usually fell off the police radar screen, he wanted to avoid an investigation into any of his more recent criminal activities and ideas. The stolen funds, a truckload of food, the planned drug deal, or the possible sale of kids. The visit to his mother would kill two birds with one stone, as she would become part of that internet scheme.

Memories of his mother had faded with time. Her protectiveness stood out, as did her forbearance of his father's adulterous, romantic behavior. She sensed Dock's need for excitement and action, and defended any problems when his father exploded at him. He forgave her one lonely reach for love and understood without explanation. It came as no surprise that Eloise owned and managed a small daycare center in her home, working with no more than eight Pre-K kids of blue-collar parents.

Dock reeked with deceit. The liquor-store murder and overwhelming knowledge of everything else he needed to hide from the police, the FBI, his bosses, the homeless…and now his mother! He'd been able to put the bad inside the good, hide the crimes within the "do-gooder" positions and jobs he'd held. From dyed blonde hair to blue contacts, his Landing disguise worked.

He could never confess to Mom, especially the murder. He'd simply have to stick with his original story He was victim of his friends' rampage and they turned on him to save themselves. Snitches! Liars! Rats!

Part of him still yearned to tell her everything, to have her hold him tightly and say, "It's okay. All is forgiven. I love you, no matter what you've done. You're my son."

Dock's latest scam grew out of an opportunistic hallway meeting at the Landing with the family of Reynaldo Alvena several weeks earlier. Alvena said, "You'll help us, sir? We lost everything."

His wife Alma said, "We spent thousands for the four of us to get here from Paraguay. We learned English. Took a special course in speaking. We got to Houston." Tears streamed down her cheeks from brown soulful eyes, finding their way to a colorful but torn polyester housedress.

Reynaldo caressed her hand. "Much money went for papers and a used truck." He twirled his mustache and then removed an old, sweat-streaked, straw cowboy hat. "Lost it all."

"Your food and beds saved us, Mr. Dock. Saved us," Alma said. "An agency even gave us clothes." She brushed off her dress.

Reynaldo said, "I've still got some dinero in my socks and shoes. Help us. Jaime is eight and Arturo is ten. We want the American dream for them...good schools, jobs, the works." He crossed himself with his hat.

Dock's mind's eye pieced it together in an instant. Sell the kids and stash them in St. Louis with his own mother. Set up a predatory child-sex trade, make a lot of money, resume contact with his mother, and then retire to a faraway beach. Of course, first buy her a house and a Cadillac.

Dock said, "Please come into my office. The boys can watch TV in the lounge."

Their sons ran to watch an old John Wayne cowboy movie dubbed in Spanish.

Once Reynaldo and Alma seated themselves near his desk, Dock pulled out a stuffed yellow envelope from the top drawer. "Take a look." He spread out samples of Social Security cards, passports, driver's licenses, and green cards.

Reynaldo stood over the desk. He slipped glasses on, then leaned over inches above the array of cards and booklets. "May I pick them up?"

"Of course," Dock said. "Show them to Alma, too."

"Yes. Yes. That's it. How much?" Reynaldo said.

"Don't worry about the money. I'll be very fair. I need classy photos of all four of you. Here's a place, the address to get them.

Tell the owner you're from here and I sent you. Give him no money. I have an arrangement. Say nothing to anyone."

"I understand," Reynaldo said. He turned to Alma and she nodded.

Reynaldo and Alma returned the next day with several sets of individual and family color shots, packaged professionally in a booklet for Dock's use. Reynaldo said, "What you wanted."

Dock sifted through them and singled out the children's pages. "Very nice of the boys. Outstanding poses in swimsuits."

"How much?" Alma said. Reynaldo glared at her.

"Well, let's see," said Dock. He wrote on a small note pad. "That's $500 for the photographs and $2,000 for the identity papers. That's for all four of you. They'll be very good quality. They'll fool everyone—police, ICE, and the other government agencies. A total of $2,500."

Reynaldo blinked. "Our truck burned with everything. Except $5,000."

"Don't worry," Dock said. "No problema. I'll take care of everything. Papers and a used pick-up truck for $3,000. Okay? It may take me weeks or even months." He hugged them both as they stood near his desk. "This is the Landing."

Reynaldo crossed himself again as he gave Dock the money. Alma kissed Dock's cheek and hugged him.

This was a sweet deal. No local partners to stab him in the back. No mules to carry drugs or risky homeless teams to sell them. No Tony. No Rocco. No Rats. Just connect with an internet predator and a child-sex ring. Show the pictures, arrange the sale and the place and time of delivery. Well, the photography studio got $250 and the forger in San Antonio now asked for $1,500. He'd find a beat-up truck for $1,250. The boys would sell for mucho dinero, since they were young, handsome, well-built, light-brown skinned, and virgins who were bi-lingual.

That evening, Dock logged into the chat room "Boy Scout Programs." He met Omar, a scoutmaster from the Midwest.

"Oh yes," said Omar, "we take these young men on vacations, camping, and hiking trips. We especially focus in the Chicago, St. Louis, and Louisville areas. We pick up the young men, supply all of their physical needs, and then return them to their destinations later. I'll e-mail you some anecdotes and testimonials. The trips cost approximately $10,000 per young man, depending on age, appearance, language skills, educational level and personal hygiene."

"I'll e-mail photos of two campers, too," Dock said. "And delivery of the campers would be in St. Louis at a daycare center."

It couldn't be this easy, so easily accessible and so readily available. Hiding in plain sight. Young boys were traded and sold over the internet as sex-slaves for 10K each. He'd won the lottery.

This time he'd get the cash first, ahead of actual delivery, just like he did with the forged identity papers. The veins in his forehead pulsed and throbbed with excitement. The hell with partners like Tony or Rocco. This time he couldn't lose.

He saved a wallet-sized photo of each boy to show to his mother. Great front views with winning smiles and only a few missing teeth. The other family photos fit nicely into a manila folder in the filing cabinet, a drawer labeled "Clients of the Landing," all very innocent and above-board. He stored pictures of other individuals and events there, to be used for newspaper or TV publicity and PR later.

Dock planned to leave for St. Louis the next day. Doubt crept into his thinking during this brief respite. So he scanned several more of the pornography chat rooms and thinly disguised child-sex web sites. Another sixty minutes on the internet and he knew with absolute certainty that he'd have no difficulty selling kids. Each child was virtually auctioned off publicly, if you read between the lines of the internet ads for services and activities.

The unwritten codes jumped out at Dock. The two Alvena boys could bring $20,000. Maybe there was a better deal than the "Boy Scouts." The chat rooms, full of pedophiles and their agents, could eventually lead the way to an even more lucrative arrangement, but the St. Louis connection with his mother was too perfect to pass up. He'd renew their relationship even if it remained long-distance. Perhaps over time he'd become a child-slavery broker, sell to the rich sheiks of the Middle East, then retire to a seaside villa in Abu Dhabi.

He packed an overnight bag with suit, shirt, glasses and toupee, made sure he had the Alvena kids' pictures, and took a cab to the Greyhound Bus Station. Too many observers and cops at the airport or even the train depot, so the slow-moving bus provided his best cover. He said, "Round trip to St. Louis, please."

The agent said, "When to leave and when to return, sir?"

"Leave tonight and return Sunday night. Just the weekend."

"Fine. That's $112.50 round trip. Your bus leaves in forty minutes at stand number four." He pushed the ticket across the counter.

Dock handed him the cash and sat down on a hard wooden bench. After five minutes, no one recognized him, then he went into the men's room and changed into his disguise and new clothes. If asked, the agent couldn't recall him as the individual who bought the tickets. He was pleased himself with the careful plans.

Once seated on the bus, overnight bag on the shelf above him, he placed his suit coat on the empty space next to him. He hadn't worn such clothes for years—really for decades. The shirt collar felt too tight, so he loosened it. Comfortable at last, the wig and goatee firmly in place, he slept.

The dream of his sisters tantalized him. There they were, both stoned and drunk, dancing a flamenco with their Latino fiancés, José and Juan, twin brothers from Puerto Rico. The girls were happy and so joyous to be engaged, caught up in their plans for weddings. As if by magic, the brothers suddenly disappeared, and his sisters danced with each other. Then his mother appeared and said, "Don't go to Starbucks tonight. I'll make coffee." Instead, they left.

Dock woke up sweating. His shirt was drenched. He couldn't see a way to go to their funerals. He had been too afraid of getting caught at that time, not nearly as secure in his job and life as now. He hoped somehow they understood and forgave him. They should have listened to Mom.

The bus finally pulled into the St. Louis station and he hailed a cab for Mom's house. Once there, he pressed the doorbell twice, as he'd done growing up.

"Oh, my God! I can't believe it. After all this time. I knew you were alive. Oh, Rod. What an outfit. Only a mother would know you." She cried and hugged and laughed and nearly collapsed, all at once.

Dock held her up and kissed the top of her head long and hard. "Love you, Mom. Sorry for the surprise. It was best this way." They hugged again and again and again. Hard and tight, then gentle and loose.

"Sure, come in. Sit down. How did you find me?" she said. She brushed off the couch pillows and fluffed them.

"Wasn't hard. You're in the book," he said. "The Eloise Mulligan Child Care Center of St. Louis."

"Your eyes and nose are the same. And your hands. They…"

Dock peeled off the mustache and goatee, then carefully removed the curly hairpiece. He slipped off his jacket, next the tie, rolled up his sleeves, smiled, and said, "Here I am. The real me."

She caressed his bleached blonde hair and ran her hands lovingly over his strong arms and shoulders. "Yes, maybe a little thinner. It's been so long, so many years."

"Nice house." He peered around the room. "You always liked comfortable chairs and couches. Guess the childcare takes place in the back."

Her skin was slightly mottled, grey hair rolled with a tight bun, and dress a bit old-fashioned but clean. She'd shrunk, too, probably several inches in height.

"Yes. In the back I've got three large rooms for kids. Had them built-on when I got the license. Toys, books, blankets, beds, potties, the works. I did it all with the money I got when your father died. He left me some money. Guilt money."

Dock's eyes brightened with a smile from ear to ear. "You deserve it. That cheapskate. By the way, they call me Dock, not Rod Mulligan. That's my name at the Landing. I'm director of a homeless shelter."

"Sounds like a very big job. You always sent me nice presents. You were afraid to get caught here."

"That's it in a nutshell. I knew you knew. Even disguise myself now, in case you didn't notice." They both chuckled, the newness and strangeness of the encounter created an awkward tension.

67

"Silly me, how about food, a shower, the spare bedroom. You'll stay?"

"Of course, I hoped you'd ask. I leave on Sunday night. What's for dinner?" He patted his stomach.

She rubbed her hands together and through her tears of joy she said, "How about pasta with marinara sauce? Simple, the way you always liked it."

"And red wine?" he said.

She nodded and went off to the kitchen. "The spare bedroom is down the hall on the left. Bathroom and shower between the rooms. Is your leg sore? You need that cane?"

Dock said, "No, no, not sore. Got a knife wound in prison. Left me with a limp."

Dock knew his capacity to survive came from her. Never re-married, she'd made her own way in the world, created her own childcare program and weathered the deaths of her ex-husband and two daughters and the long estrangement of her only son. Such a survivor had much to teach the homeless, who traded too often on a revolving, escapist, pity-party of food, housing, drugs, booze, sickness, and craziness. Tough old bird, that Eloise Mulligan.

Dock showered, cleaned the sticky glue off of his face, hung up his suit, and slipped on flip-flops, then shorts, and a t-shirt. "Home sweet home," he said to no one in particular. "No matter how far you roam..."

Eloise called, "Pasta's ready and hot. Just like you always loved it. Said it reminded you of your Italian buddies. See how I re-member?" She ladled it into two huge bowls.

The phone rang. "Yes, this is Eloise. Oh, hello, Martha. You'll never guess what's happened!"

Dock arose, then placed his right hand lightly over her mouth and the left index finger near his lips. "Don't mention me."

Eloise nodded. "I've got to go, Martha. Call you in the morning. Hot stuff on the stove. Bye, dear."

They sat twirling and chewing pasta and drinking red table wine. Eloise said, "I freeze containers of the marinara sauce, just in case I need it quickly. The jug wine is all I can afford."

"It's just great. I always loved playing with long spaghetti. Just great," Dock said. "We've got all tomorrow to reminisce…to talk about the family, and everything that's happened to us. After prison, I changed my identity and worked in several non-profits in Dallas, then took over as director of a new homeless shelter called the Landing."

Eloise left the room for a moment and returned with a framed picture of Dock. She placed it on the table. "Your high school graduation. Remember? I was so proud of you then and I'm so proud of you now. They wouldn't still care about the parole thing would they?"

"Yes, I'm afraid they would. Tonight, tonight I need to tell you about a way we can see each other from time-to-time and actually work together on an important project." Dock circled the tiny dining room, glanced at the photo, and ran his fingers over the dark, highly polished furniture he remembered as a child. He'd carved his initials in the back of the china cabinet. It was still there. R.M.

She poured another glass of the red table wine. "We're a lot alike. We both help kids and their parents. I got an associate's degree when I opened my own center. I don't charge as much as I could." Her loving gaze devoured him.

Dock, mildly embarrassed, sat down and sipped his drink. "Many of the kids at my center, homeless kids, get adopted or put in foster care. Parents who are illegal immigrants, with no papers, want their kids to have American colleges and American healthcare. They let some of their kids get adopted out, and become children of U.S. parents. No one checks very closely."

"They must love their kids so much to sacrifice like that. Pure parental love."

"Yes, they give their kids a shot at the American dream. Later on, the kids sometimes feel guilty or ashamed of their status. They know they weren't born here. Of course, their adopting parents don't always want to know the whole story, either."

Eloise picked up the dirty dishes and placed them in one side of the small kitchen sink. "How do we work together? What's the project?"

"Well, glad you asked. You've always been there for me."

69

"Yes, but that high-priced lawyer I paid for couldn't get you out of prison soon enough to suit me." She dried her hands and sat across from Dock again.

"For now, you can house a few of my kids at your center. Sometimes a day or two, sometimes several weeks at the most. Then a lawyer, or parent, or the county will pick them up. I'll pay per diem to you for each kid. That should help."

"Sounds good." She smiled and patted his hand.

"Some of the kids may not speak very good English. Only Spanish or possibly Portuguese. Okay?" He opened his wallet. "These are pictures of Jaime and Arturo, probably the first."

"Muy bueno," Eloise said. She stood behind him and threw her arms around Dock. Then she picked up the pictures. "Muy bueno, my Rod. Handsome boys, like you."

Dock said, "Being here reminds me of Dad. We knew about him. My sisters knew. I knew, even when I was a little boy."

Eloise's shoulders slumped as she sat again. She smoothed a few loose gray hairs. "I should have. I guess in a way, I did know. I usually blotted it out of my mind."

"We knew about you, too," Dock said. "That once."

"The girls forgave me. I was so lonely then and upset when I met this guy. He was lonesome and needed me. We were together once. I guess I got even."

"Dad lied a lot when you split-up." He pushed back his chair and stood near his mother, slid both arms around her. "I never forgave him for being a snitch during the divorce. Never will."

When Eloise arose suddenly, she blew Dock a kiss, and rushed into her room, covering her face with both hands. "Tomorrow," she said. "Plenty of time, tomorrow."

All the ingredients in Dock's new scheme fell neatly into place. When he returned to the Landing, he'd carefully arrange the abduction and the internet sale of the Alvena boys. The when, how, and the method of payment. The boys would stay with his mother when the sale and exchange went down. She loved children. He'd sleep well tonight, feeling safer and more loved than he could remember, certain that no evidence linked him to any of his criminal activity, past, present, or future.

His mother knocked on the door. "There's one more thing," she said. "Please come out."

They both sat at the table again.

"More wine?" she asked.

"No. What's up?"

She pushed her chair close to his and gazed directly at his eyes. Her brown eyes and his green blended into a hazel in the candle-light. "I've got a secret."

"Can it wait until breakfast?"

"No, now or never." She hung her head and her body shook with pain. "You've got a brother, Dock, a half-brother."

"Come on, Mom. That's quite a statement." Dock stood and fidgeted with his hands as he walked around the table several times. "You must be kidding."

"It's true. Do you want to hear the story?"

Dock put his hands on his ears. "Not really."

"Well, when you were about ten years old, I got fed up with your father's women and booze and went to a bar one night. I just wanted to drown my sorrows."

"So?"

"I met a guy and we drank and danced and had fun." She moved her arms and torso rhythmically in synchrony with the memory of some long-ago big band melody. "Then we went to a motel and had sex. My first, except for your father."

Dock didn't know whether to laugh or cry. She told him much more than he wanted to know. "Where's the brother part fit in?" Still stunned by her confession, he already knew the answer.

"The man was a military guy in uniform. He said it was his first time to cheat and I believed him. Great sex, the delusion of love, and escape for a few hours. In our defense, we were very, very drunk."

"Mom, it's okay. We all make mistakes. God knows, I have." He tenderly wiped away her tears with his handkerchief.

She sobbed with tortured breathing. Finally, she vomited the pasta into a cup. "I got pregnant."

He held her shaking frame. Now he realized how bent and bro-ken her body was, much weaker than he remembered. "It's okay.

71

It's all right."

"The African-American sergeant, a really, really good guy admitted he was the father and pledged to take care of his son Kip… your half-brother."

"That was his name?"

His mother relaxed for a moment, her body nearly limp. "That was his nickname from the start. Your mother gave birth to a half-black son from a one-night stand. Christian name Kendrick."

"Do you mean Kip Crandall?"

"Yes, that's it."

"I left you and the girls and your father for several months and gave birth to Kip. The sergeant and his wife raised him, he was a light-skinned, handsome boy. I know because I followed them to their home from the hospital and found out their name and address." She sat upright now and dried her eyes.

"My God, that's the guy who's been asking questions at the Landing! Used to be a cop," Dock said. "That fucker, sorry, Mom, is my half-brother. You and a black soldier. That's just plain crazy and horrible. Brother spies on brother. Too much to swallow. You must be mistaken."

"I'm not. Those are the facts. He had a younger brother who died in jail."

"Have you told him? Do you know him? Have you spoken to him or the sergeant's family?"

"No," she said, "and I never will. It's over for me. They gave him a good home."

"Do you understand that I know him? You heard me?"

"Yes, I do," she said. Then she stood and straightened her back, wiped her eyes again, smoothed her hair, and walked toward her bedroom. "Sorry to spill all these beans. I had to do it."

Dock said, "It's such a surprise. Such a coincidence. I'll deal with it."

"I know you will," she said. "Your sisters never knew. Your dad didn't know. I covered it up. The Sergeant was a real gentleman. I don't know what he told his wife. He probably sold her on the idea of a bi-racial infant son. Maybe she even knew the truth, but I doubt it."

"I'm glad you told me. You trust me." Dock hugged her again.

She said, "Yes. So much shame and guilt all these years. I had to tell you. I just had to before I died."

Dock said, "No more of that." He kissed her forehead. "Sleep tight."

He poured himself another glass of wine. How could he use this discovery? Could he blackmail Kip? The booze and that gay Marty. Could he throw the episode at him?

They never told Kip. Seemed implausible. Kip and Dock, and the same mother. Maybe Mom had some of the facts mixed-up. She had aged! In his gut he felt like Kip would help him if the chips were down. Maybe there was something between them beyond blood. His mind still whirred with this news, gradually shut down by the power of many glasses of wine. He had to concentrate on the drug deal. That was priority número uno.

Chapter Eight

Despite Kip's best efforts to rehabilitate himself and his professional life, unfinished business reared its ugly head, especially after half a liter of vodka and a thin-crust pepperoni pizza. Kip tried to avoid these dark hours, but didn't always succeed. He thought his mixed heritage, though never mentioned, helped get him the undercover job at the Landing. There was diversity at the Landing, but the majority was white not black, brown, or red. Was it a perverse sort of affirmative action or just racism? Hire a black man to clean up and do the dirty work. He had his doubts, threats to his self-esteem, as all the legitimate questions concerning his preparations and readiness for the new assignment re-surfaced painfully in his mind

He could be a better leader than Dock. Dock, a phony and hypocrite. Dock, probably a drug dealer. Dock, likely a petty crook who stole money from a Salvation Army kettle and fresh food destined for a soup kitchen.

Why the obsession? Why so much thought and worry and curiosity about Dock? What did Dock mean to him? Who was Dock?

And who was Kip? He couldn't put his finger on it but there always seemed to be a connection to Dock. Both hid from others, were helpful, yet remained unmarried and had no kids.

Dock was the bad boy whom society sacrificed The criminal, the rule-breaker, the anti-social guy camouflaged in the cloth of a do-gooder.

Kip hurt himself, drank, left the police force, remained stuck in grief and punished himself, called himself a mutt, failed to treasure his divine existence. Was he the highly ethical conscience of society, the true sentinel and guardian of others, also hiding something sinister and evil?

Being a cop allowed Kip to submerge the dark side that wanted to punish Dock for what he'd done. Yet the other side, the compassionate part, knew he would warn Dock, and in that way try to help him survive. He couldn't harm him, but he couldn't become a close friend, either.

It sounded corny, but cops need a crook and crooks need a cop. Cops deny the crook inside, and crooks avoid the deeply buried cop. Life became so complicated, too confusing for Kip to cope with sober. Something to ease the pain, to feel good and whole and straightforward became necessary for him. The Serenity Prayer didn't always suffice.

So he downed another stiff drink, Russian vodka, no ice, just like the Czars. "That's more like it."

His cell phone rang. "Hi, Kip. It's Bill here. Just thinking about you."

Kip dropped the glass, which broke, quietly caught in the act by Bill's surprise call. It was 11:00 p.m. on a Friday night.

"Hi, Bill. Doing some self-medication." He poured a fresh tumbler and set it on a table near him.

"The demons again? Past, present, or future?"

Kip said, "All of the above. A real slip tonight. I think I need that pill for a few months. Make myself sick as hell when I touch alcohol."

Bill said, "You'd have to remember to take one of them every day. Would you?"

Kip grabbed the tumbler of crystal clear magic and held it to the ceiling light. "I'd try. One day at a time."

"No time for jokes," said Bill. "Do you want me to come over to your place? I can be there in an hour or so."

"Just talk to me. The bottle's empty now, so that's it for tonight." He drained the tumbler.

Bill said, "Talk is cheap. What's on your mind? Can you forgive this slip? It's been three months sober for you."

Kip said, "I've got to." He stumbled over a stack of pizza boxes and fell onto the couch.

"Start going to more meetings. I seldom see you there."

"Well, yes, but I'm so busy with my job." Okay, it sounded like a stupid excuse, he pounded the cushion with venom.

"You have time to drink. You're called a functional alcoholic.

The rest is bullshit. Unless you moved to another…"

"Oh, no," said Kip. "My life is definitely here." He stood and kicked the empty bottle to the end of the room.

"So, what's it going to be?"

"I can't stop thinking of Wendy. Why her? She suffered so much at the end. She cried all the time with the pain." Kip sobbed quietly. "The morphine hardly touched it. I tried to find a way, but all I did was hold her and tell her I loved her."

"You know, Wendy loved California. The cloudless, sun and warm water in the south and the giant redwoods' shadows of the north. She skied in the snowy mountains near L.A., then hiked in the forests near Oregon with her parents. Memories from her childhood always remained fresh and vivid. She wanted to conceive our first child in California, to always remember another wonderful, special moment from there.

Just before my lieutenant's exam, I took Wendy to California for a four day excursion. Sergeant Kip Crandall, father-to-be, so virile yet loving, drove all the way to the Bay Area with Wendy, mother-to-be. We were in our early thirties, and both of us wanted a child, and then another and another!"

"Wendy said, 'Would twenty be too many?'

"I said, 'In a three-bedroom? Kind of crowded, don't you think?'

"I drove with one arm hugging her and the other hand on the steering wheel of our used Buick. She named it the Guzzler.

"We found a motel in the foothills near San Gregorio Beach on that winding road to Santa Cruz, then stopped for the night. Exhausted by the drive, we immediately fell asleep in our clothes, too tired to undress or shower.

"I had a dream, so impossible to forget, which forged an even closer bond between us. We wore white swimsuits, hands entwined, as we navigated a rocky hillside that led directly to the sandy shore. Above us, on a craggy promenade someone observed us with binoculars.

"'Let's put on a show,' said Wendy.

"We wrestled each other to the sand, rolled and jostled into the shallow water's edge. Ripping off our trunks and bikini top, our bodies melted together seamlessly, warm kisses and light, gentle strokes of skin, water and sand smoothing the movements.

"'Your lips are so perfect. I love you. Your hair, your arms, your legs. ' I said.

"'Oh, yes, my darling. You're wonderful.'

"At last, the tide stirred us back to consciousness.

"'I'm embarrassed,' Wendy said as she slid her suit on. 'Someone watched.'

"I picked her up and carried her up the steep hill. Me, Tarzan, you, Jane.

"The dream ended, we awoke in the motel that morning refreshed by sleep and the clean, salty air. We kissed and made love. Then we finally showered and dressed.

"Wendy said, 'Let's walk on the beach.'

"I didn't mention the dream to Wendy. She was dead four months later.

"Now I treasure the dream, reliving it frequently, for what it was and what might have been in a better world. My joy outweighs the sadness and loss increasingly as time passes by.

"I never did understand who watched us from the hillside. Sometimes, I thought it might have been God, knowing full well the heartbreak that lay ahead."

Bill said, "You do have a God, your higher power, so be realistic. You're just a man. Have some faith in Him and yourself."

"You know just what to say, Bill. Are you sure you're a factory worker?"

Bill said, "What else you worried about? Go to more meetings before you get prescribed medication. You do good on the job."

"Fuck it." He threw a pizza box at the window. Then he picked up the vodka bottle, turned it upside down, let the few drops fall to the floor, and shattered it against the old brick fireplace.

Bill said, "What the hell?"

"Just some light housecleaning," Kip said. "You know I didn't really do much for Larry. He got into drugs big-time while I was in the service. I came home and found him a real mess. He hung himself in jail."

Bill said, "Forgive and forget. That was a long time ago. If you can't, or won't, forgive yourself, no one else can do it for you. So?"

Kip ruminated on that message. Faith in your higher power. Know yourself, help yourself, forgive yourself. All that, after you declare emotional bankruptcy, your own helplessness and failure in the face of addiction. It made sense, with a kind of twisted logic that doubled back on itself. To you, to me, to the individual. Kind of an emotional boomerang.

"You still there?" Bill asked.

"Just thinking. I'm making coffee now. Black and hot and thick in my new espresso machine. Lots of sugar, too."

"What else?"

"Nothing really new," Kip said. "There were my mentees while I volunteered at the Landing. Namey, Squeaky, and Tottie who is a long-term project, with some possibility."

"Shit, man, you got medical attention for Squeaky, and Namey was a total druggie whack job, before, during, and after you. Get your facts straight," Bill said. "I probably couldn't become a cop or an Army MP. I've only got a late-life fucking GED and I machine hood clamps for tractors all day long. Ain't no miracles in this shitty world unless God says there are. Got it?"

"Yes, I do."

"Okay, here's the real deal. Ninety meetings in ninety days. Start all over. Don't go to the AA group at the Landing. Go somewhere else. It'll be better. Don't drink with your ex-partner or other women. Don't marry for at least a year. Addict love is not good for you. Not yet."

"Okay, but I won't stay away from women," Kip said. He poured espresso into a big white cup.

"Your choice, your chance. Got to go to work, I'm late for second shift." He hung up.

Kip said, "Thanks," to a dead line. He needed more coffee, then a lot of sleep.

He slid into bed, full of vodka and espresso and finally fell into a self-medicated sleep. Not drunk, not sober, half and half, like his life…who was he….never free of doubt and uncertainty, never completely sure of himself. He'd put on tough airs as a cop and PI, taken courageous stands at times, but still…

The long, complicated dream started with a night-time fishing expedition. Squeaky, Namey, and Tottie in a bass boat with Kip steering the outboard motor. All had lines in the water with jiggly, gummy lures that large-mouth bass sucked up. Kip, drunk and nearly delirious, directed the boat in a huge figure eight. Too fast to catch many fish, but slow enough to create a perfect design in the water.

He said "We moved eight times while my dad was in the army. Eight times to a new place, new friends, new schools, new everything. I never really knew who I was or even where I was, long enough to have a home."

Squeaky dropped his rod and reel into the water, lit a cigarette, and coughed. His body erupted into flames and smoke as he fell overboard and disappeared. Namey dove after him into the murky, brackish water sprinkled with huge green lily pads, but didn't surface again. Both gone.

Tottie screamed and cried, "They're dead! I've got a fish!"

Kip reeled in the small, shiny black-green bass on Tottie's line. "It will be okay. They lived their own lives. Both vets."

"Squeaky built look-out camps in the mountains of Cambodia. Not very bright, with few leadership skills, his combat engineer training didn't pay off in civilian life.

"Namey's survivor's guilt resulted from his whole squad being blown up in their Humvee in Iraq. His training as a mechanic couldn't counterbalance the continued use of drugs, especially meth, since his deployment in the Middle East. Then his PTSD and lousy, brief marriage."

I understand enough of that to know I want to be different. I want to live a good life," Tottie said.

"It's very difficult to walk a different path, but it should be easier for you now than when you're my age. I'll help you as much as I can," Kip said.

They shook hands.

Tottie said, "You look blacker."

Kip put his right arm around Tottie's shoulders and steered the boat toward shore with his left hand.

Tottie said, "I go to school now." He gave a thumbs-up sign.

"I've got an idea. Once we get married in a year or so, how would you like to live with Karen and me and the girls? You know, try it out?"

Tottie asked, "Sleep at your house?"

Kip said, "More than that. Be a member of a family. Maybe we'd adopt you."

"Sounds good. I could always leave, couldn't I? " He struggled to get the hook out of the fish's mouth.

"Of course," Kip said. He hugged him so hard that the boat nearly capsized. Tears of happiness mixed with the frothy mist created by the motor.

Kip's real roots, the permanent home he'd missed while growing up, were finally planted when he married Wendy. They met at a friend's house. She, a nurse, and he, a young cop. Her parents were dead, but his were still alive and threw them a blockbuster church wedding and party.

There she stood at the shoreline as he backed the boat into its slip. She asked, "Hi, honey, have a good time?" Wendy looked lovely in white shorts and a pink halter, showing off her long red hair.

Then she disappeared. Gone without a word of goodbye, or love, or thanks. Simply not there, as if the cancer had abruptly eaten her alive, and left nothing but memories.

Kip awakened with a start, for a moment not sure what was dream and what was real. He felt calm and relaxed, searched for tears on the pillow, but it was dry.

He remembered that he had a date for dinner that night. They'd eat somewhere that did not have a bar, not even a BYOB joint.

For some inexplicable reason, his obsession with Dock took hold again and grew, even after a hot shower and black coffee. He'd nail that crook if it was the last thing he did. He jerked open the window blinds to a blazing sun that drenched him with hope.

Chapter Nine

"You can call me, Pete. I'm Pedro Lopez Menuto. Call me Pete." In a new Rangers' sweatshirt with white turtleneck, matched by red and white sport shoes, he could pass for a thirty-year-old tourist from Monterrey in town to see a baseball game.

"Well now, Pete, everyone here calls me Dock. It's a nickname. I bring hope to the homeless. Care for a drink?"

"Kind of a shitty office for the boss to have, isn't it?" Pete touched a few books in a library rack, next moved to the window. "You sure there's no bugs or recorders going? If there are, you're dead, Dock. Very dead."

Dock said, "Oh no, I assure you. We're quite alone and safe. I'm honored by your personal visit. Please make yourself comfortable."

"Where's the $50,000, my gringo friend? Mi amigo."

Dock dropped a large brown paper bag on the desktop. "It's all here. Every last penny." He smirked. "It's a federal-government award to help my homeless flock."

Pete said, "Homeless, my ass. Dump it."

Dock opened the bag and spread the cash out neatly so Pete could see it. "Take a look."

"Good. Good." Pete scooped up the cash, counted it, and put it back in the bag. "Now you listen real good. The product will be in clear plastic bags inside pillows and mattresses. Comes from a factory outside of Mexico City. A truck will drop it off here tomorrow. Rocco and Tony will receive it at the loading ramp in back. Then we're even. Got it." He stood and wiped new Ray-Ban designer sunglasses with a red Italian silk handkerchief.

"Yes, sounds perfect to me. You can keep the cash at delivery time. We'll store the pillows and mattresses inside our supplies area. No one else will touch it." Dock held the office door open for Pete. He reached for the bag but Pete kept it.

"This is a drop in the bucket," Pete said. "More money, more drugs. Next time will be a much bigger deal. Then my people will know you're a stand-up gringo we can count on. I'd hate to see your head delivered here in a suitcase." Sack in hand, he swaggered through the hall.

Dock said, "One question. What's your cartel?"

Pete walked on. "Don't you trust me?" He twirled a straight-razor in his free hand as he kicked the door open to the parking lot, and disappeared.

Rocco and Tony barged into Dock's office, arrogantly settling into two armchairs.

"So?" Tony said.

"Is it on?" Rocco said.

"Yes. Yes. Yes," Dock said. "We're in business. I gave him the $50,000 and they'll deliver it tomorrow to our receiving area. Maybe I was careless with the money, but Pete is a stand-up guy. We can count on him."

"Our cut?" Rocco said.

"Yes. I'll give you each one-third." He showed one finger on his left hand and three fingers on the right.

"That's what I'm talking about, Dock. You're the boss," Tony said.

Rocco stood tall. "We'll keep our mouths zipped up tight." He ran a finger over his lips.

"I know I can count on you both," Dock said. "When the product comes, store it and mark it, 'Do not touch, personal and confidential.' Tape the boxes so no one knows that the pillows and the mattresses are there."

"When do we get the product out?" Rocco said.

Dock said, "We'll make sure the product is there, that we've gotten what we paid for. Then we'll have our staff meeting and decide who goes where…Houston, Chicago, Detroit, even Toledo. Right up the middle."

Tony rubbed his hands together briskly, a slight sweat appearing on his huge forehead. He took off his tall chef's cap and mopped his head with his sleeve. "I can taste it."

Rocco said, "Our guys don't know details. Just give them packages or bags that look like the usual shit the homeless carry. Then they deliver and bring us back the money. If they don't, they know they're dead." He scratched his neck. "Me, I'm getting a real thick gold chain with a diamond cross."

Dock nodded. "Excuse my French, but these dumb fucks don't know what they're carrying. They can guess all they want. Our staff includes Buster, Squeaky, Namey, and Queenie, and several kids like Tottie. If they lie, they die." He slid his hand quickly over his throat.

Tony said, "We should make five times what we paid. Right?"

"Approximately, depending on unforeseen expenses." Dock thumbed through some papers on his desk. "See you both in Receiving tomorrow evening."

The next night at 8:00 p.m. sharp, the three met again. The Receiving area held huge, swinging doors above a ramp so trucks could unload easily. Tucked away from sight behind wire fence walls stood three large cardboard boxes marked: "Do Not Touch," and "Destination los Estados Unidos."

"Hurry up, boss, we can't wait. The assholes, I mean our staff, will be here at 10:00 p.m. for training and their assignments," Tony said. "We got to go over stuff before they arrive."

Dock hesitated, then limped slowly into Receiving, never one to be ordered around by the hired help. He was in charge, not Tony and not Rocco. His planning skills determined the what, when, why, and wherefores. He considered himself the managing general partner.

He pulled out a box-cutter for each of them. "Go ahead, check it out." Raw excitement added to the tension always present when the partners met. "Make sure it's all there."

Tony wrestled a box and slit it down the side. He accidentally cut a pillow, but no matter since they intended eventually to open all of the pillows and mattresses. He shook the pillow, and a plastic bag stuffed with confetti slipped out. "Big joke, boss." Then he hurriedly sliced open two more pillows and mattresses, paper stuffing falling everywhere, covering up the bubble packaging material. "It's all bullshit. Those fuckers. No product."

Rocco said, "They stiffed us, Dock. Took the money but no

product. Do they think we're homeless imbeciles?" He pounded the remaining boxes until they cracked open.

Tony and Rocco rolled around on the floor throwing pillows and mattress sections at each other.

Dock checked the other two boxes. "Nothing here either. I was cocksure about this deal. Pete will pay for this. Big time. He and his group, no matter who they are." He punched his fist into a chunk of mattress and kicked a box into the wall. "Tell our staff there's been a change, cancel the meeting and clean up this mess." He stomped out as fast as his bad leg would let him.

Dock headed straight for his office. He grabbed the cell phone Pete had given him. An emergency number rang several times before Pete spoke. "Si, what is it?"

Dock said, "You fucked us. I want my money back, got that, Slick."

Pete said, "Sorry, mi amigo, no can do. Boss felt you weren't a good risk. Homeless people get robbed, or beaten, and killed. They drug and drink. Too much of a chance."

Dock said, "So that's it. You keep the fifty and..."

"Yes," Pete said, "and you keep the pillows and mattresses. Sleep well, my friend. Remember, if you try to get your money, we'll burn down your place. Your head in a suitcase. You're an ex-con, baby." The line went dead.

Dock poured himself a double-rye and water, exhaled a huge sigh, and literally fell into his chair. "How did they know?" he asked.

Tony and Rocco stormed into the office. Dock said, "Pour your-selves a stiff drink. I've got some very bad news." Tony poured the rye while Rocco added water. All three chug-a-lugged.

"Gentlemen, in your vernacular, we have been fucked over, royally screwed, taken a big one up the ass, and so on and so forth. If we go after the money, they'll burn the Landing and kill us. Somehow they know I've had my share of...."

"You got to do something," said Tony. "You stole the $50,000, but we're still out all the profit. Lot of money to lose. This was the start of a successful business. Can't just say fuck it."

Rocco spoke in measured tones. "I'd hate to see you back down, Dock. You've got to be tough."

"I need time to think. I'll find Pete," Dock said. He tried to control the shakes.

Tony said, "Shit, it might be..."

"All I had was a phone number. I'll get him," Dock said.

Tony finished a second drink. "You better do that, boss. We can't be had like this. Word will get out we're patsies." He raised his glass as if to pitch it against the wall then lowered it. "You're really a dumb fuck. You know what we do with dumb fucks."

Dock had a peculiar kind of trust in others. Even so, he knew Rocco and Tony didn't have his back. They wouldn't protect him if he needed it and couldn't be trusted any more than Pete. They'd turn on him. They'd snitch. They'd rat him out. They might even be in on it. Both had to die!

Dock poured another drink. He said, "Don't worry, partners. We'll have one-third each. I'll take care of it. We'll make big bread. Tony, you'll never have to cook again."

The deal went sour, so things changed. The party planned for late that night to celebrate a successful drug deal was cancelled. Originally, Dock, Tony, and Rocco, and selected homeless residents were to be feted at a champagne dinner. Instead, the partners met for a quiet, private dinner at Rocco's condo.

Dock knew the lay-out, the two-bedroom reflected the viewpoint of a decorator asked to furnish the place as cheaply as possible, capturing the aura of a Tuscan villa. Fake marble columns, huge vases overflowing with artificial flowers and imitation dark antiques crowded the living room. The single comfortable place was the master bathroom, left largely untouched because of going over-budget on the kitchen.

A round dining-room table allowed the five of them to see each other as Rocco, Maryanne, Tony, Teri, and Dock ate and drank and talked.

Teri said, "If I have another drink, I'll dance." She wiggled her butt.

"The hell you will," Tony said. "You show your titties plenty."

"Her ass, too," Rocco said.

Dock arose and poured a drinkable Il Tesoro Chianti into each wineglass. He accidentally brushed the neck of Teri as he passed her chair.

"Ooo, la la," she said. "Dock, I didn't know you cared."

Maryanne said, "You know, Dock, you're not half-bad looking and you're more educated than any of us. What about a wife? It'd be more fun with six of us."

Dock said, "You're right. It's time. I've got a good job, solid future, and enough money to support a wife and kids, even a home with a white-picket fence."

"Jesus, Dock," Tony said. He gulped down the wine.

Rocco raised his glass in a toast. "What Tony means is it sounds good, Dock, so do it. Then it'd always have to be a third each, right? We'd all be married and equal shares, the same."

Dock grinned. "That's mixing apples and oranges, Rocco, if you can get them. Marriage with executive brain power. They don't mix."

"Come on, everybody." Tony nearly emptied the bottle into his glass. "Bottoms up. It don't get no better than this. We're partners."

Teri leaned over to Dock and rubbed his shoulders with both hands. "If I can't dance at least I can massage."

He pulled away and poured more wine. "Okay if I open another bottle?"

"Hell yes, we're partners," Rocco said.

Dock said, "That lasagna sauce was fabulous, Maryanne. I get fed up with Tony's bland cooking at the Landing."

Tony spilled some wine. "Shove it, Dock. Think you could do any better? Fuck them powdered eggs, sacks of potatoes full of holes, rice that's ten years old from government warehouses?"

"Take it easy. Just pulling your chain." Dock clinked wine glasses with Tony. "To you, big boy, the best chef the center ever had."

Rocco said, "You girls know that we're all partners now in a business deal. Dock's the boss. There's plenty for everybody."

Teri moved rhythmically from the waist up, side-to-side while waving her hands. "Oh, goody. We'll be rich. Can we buy our own club? I want a bookcase full of porn videos."

Dock said, "Not so fast, people. Don't talk about this outside of our little family here. Okay?"

Four heads nodded.

Tony said, "You know we can keep a secret. We've got the goods on each other, don't we?"

Teri said, "If we're rich, then…"

Dock said, "Just a second. If you didn't have much, say you're an Amazon River native and you lose half, you didn't lose much. If you had ten million and lose half, you lose a lot."

"So, you're still rich with millions." Teri arched her back in triumph.

Maryanne said, "But things you want today, maybe even need, could be in such short supply. Big boats, private planes, huge houses, fancy cars. Oh, Teri, you are so childish and stupid."

Teri said, "I'd rather have five million of not much stuff here than one-half of nothing in a rainforest. I don't like monkey meat or boiled wild fruit leaves." She shook her torso again. "By the way, Maryanne, you could use more makeup and less weight."

Dock said, "Don't forget about the pain, real hot, intense, bloody pain. If you lose one-half again, you're down to two and a half million. That's pain, insufferable pain, with nothing to change its course." His tone was that of a Socratic schoolmaster, impatient with his students.

Rocco said, "You people are too serious. Too fucking serious. We've got a perfect cover here. Our business deal runs through the center and the homeless work for us. We'll change a few things. Dock will do it."

"Let's stand and hold hands for a moment," Maryanne said. They rose and bowed heads. "Dear Lord, thanks for this bountiful meal, for the fellowship and love of our dear friend and family, for all you've done for us. And especially for helping us hide our little secrets."

Tony's huge body nearly slid out of his chair. He said, "Little secrets, my ass."

Dock said, "If we tell each other the whole truth, no one can use it on the other one. We're all in it together, till death do us part."

Tony said, "Yeah, like seeing your friends in a cathouse. Nobody snitches."

Rocco said, "Boss, how come you don't ever take anything from any of them? Have your car washed or your apartment cleaned?" He shook his closed right hand as if rolling a pair of dice, then flicked it up.

Dock stood and faced the window. "Well, I did some criminal things a long time ago. I'll never go back to prison. I'd rather die first."

Tony asked, "Bad shit?"

"During college, I joined an armed robbery of a liquor store. Two buddies said they needed a driver and that I'd get a full share if I drove. Unfortunately, the store owner died after being shot in the stomach twice. My buddy Giovanni testified against me. He got a reduced sentence of twenty-five years for his false testimony that I was the shooter and supplied the .357 magnum. My attorney pled me to armed robbery, and I was out of prison in three."

Maryanne said, "What happened next, Dock?"

"Well, I left New York, violated parole, and changed my appearance. At thirty, with my hair dyed blonde, eyes blue with contacts, my trim neat appearance landed me a job for room and board as the director of the Soup Kitchen at St. Francis, then next, to the Salvation Army Kitchen and eventually became director of the Landing at age fifty."

Tony asked, "How in the hell did you get these jobs with a felony conviction and prison and all?"

"They weren't thorough." He slapped himself on the shoulder several times. "I was lucky. The non-profits checked me out financially and medically, but only went to the state criminal database. I'm clean here with a good work record in Texas."

Tony and Rocco exchanged glances, the same question in each pair of untrusting, unblinking mobster eyes. They clinked glasses, and chug-a-lugged their wine.

Tony twisted into his chair slowly. "I guess confession is good for the soul. Rocco and me, well, we both had pretty high-up jobs. So did Maryanne. Two different crime families in New York. Me and him and Teri and Maryanne, we're in the FBI's Witness Pro-tection Program."

Dock said, "I'll be damned." He clapped his hands slowly.

Rocco said, "Guess we're birds of a feather except we didn't serve no time. We snitched on guys above us so they went away for a long, long time." He rolled his eyes for emphasis. "By the way, that Marty and Kip at the center are FBI types. Just nosing around, looking for something."

Dock popped the cork on a fresh bottle of wine. "I know."

Tony held the bottle high and said, "To the future. God, I miss the past. Now it's toothless hags in a homeless shelter kitchen. I used to have respect. I killed people."

Rocco almost fell over with laughter. "I used to eat spaghetti off of hookers' tits and then shoot craps. Shit, I miss it." He glanced at Maryanne. "Honey, way before we were married."

Dock said, "Behave yourselves, guys and gals. Keep your, I mean our mouths shut. This discussion never happened."

"Right, boss," Rocco said.

Tony nodded several times, his thick neck nearly bursting open from the fat encircling purple veins. "We all got something in common...we're fucking criminals. Homeless shelter staff, my ass. We've got a great place to hide out."

Teri and Maryanne clinked glasses and couldn't restrain their smug, proud joy. Maryanne said, "Birds of a feather."

Dock couldn't trust any of them. They were rats, just like his dad and Giovanni. If he failed to find Pete, these two mobsters would get him. He pulled out his snub-nosed .38 detective special. He darted quickly around the table and shot each person once in the back of the head. Such a sudden unexpected movement took all by surprise, even these seasoned crime-family members. Bright red blood spurted over the food and wine. Heads jerked back-ward, then bowed as they thudded onto the table.

"So long, rats. I hate rats. You thought you'd saved yourselves. You got exactly what you deserved. They'll blame the mob."

He slipped on rubber gloves and washed his plate, silverware, and wine glass carefully, then put them into the proper kitchen cabinets. He wiped areas he'd touched with a cotton cloth, the chair, table, and wine bottle. He artfully re-arranged the dining table with only four place settings and chairs. Dinner for four. Two center-volunteers and their wives murdered. Only crime families would reach back into time and kill such witnesses.

Dock limped leisurely back to his apartment. The brief, hot rain failed to cool anything or provide even a short respite from the heat. The wet residue of bacteria, fungi, mold, and pungent odors grew outside where the homeless slept. Yes, better to have at least a poncho, or a roof over your head when it rained, than a dripping bridge or tent with holes or a broken umbrella that leaked. Strangely, he thought of stripping to the waist to enjoy the downpour.

Dock always preferred hurricanes to calm seas. Genuine thrills of a carnival ride or the risks and dangers of shoplifting when he was in eighth grade. Never caught by shop owners or police, he considered himself both very lucky and invincible. His family preached right and wrong, solid moral values and his sisters were "saints" according to his parents.

Still, he preferred the "bad boy" image, attracted to the "wrong crowd" from the "other side of the tracks." His friends and acquaintances mostly belonged to gangs, some Hispanic, a few black, but usually Italian. He prized his freedom and independence, friendly to all but truly loyal to none. He paddled a one-man kayak.

Dock hummed a childhood lullaby as he turned the radio in his apartment to the Friday night symphony. He lay down on the couch to nap. He quickly sat up and pulled off his wet clothes and toweled away the dampness. He felt safe with Tony and Rocco gone. There would be no evidence linking him to the murders. The huge window fan whirred him into sleep.

He dreamt of a reunion with his mother on a cruise ship, without the fear of getting caught by the police or FBI. She always had his back. She said, "I'm not sure I can save you this time. Even Mom can fail."

Chapter Ten

Kip drove slowly, feeling relaxed away from the Landing. The undercover "acting," to pretend all the time to live on the street, took its psychic toll. He and Marty shed their homeless garb, showered, then headed out for pizza and beer in fresh clothes.

Marty gave up silver jewelry along with her dark hair. Two inch hoops now dangled loosely from each ear, eighteen-carat gold to match her new blonde doo. She was ready for her flight to Detroit to see her wife and child. "That goddamn Irish broad Maryanne thinks she's a Wall Street genius."

Kip nodded. "Yeah, not really Irish, but Maryanne's definitely a know-it-all. She was near the top of the mob family, actually made their investments."

Marty said, "Bet that's the last mob woman who gets up off her backside. She tattle-taled plenty to the Bureau. How about Rocco and his hot tamale?"

Kip rolled his eyes seductively. "She's something. Looks like a Dallas Cowboys cheerleader with a six-grade education. I'm told Rocco and Teri are behaving now. I'm concerned what she'll say in bed with some John, while too much cheap champagne gurgles around inside those fantastic flat abs."

After stuffing themselves on pepperoni and mushroom thin crust and Shiner Bock, they drove home. Kip turned right and into the driveway of the small duplex bungalow they rented. Marty often flew back to Detroit on weekends to be with her son and her wife, the English professor. He'd be alone as usual except for the extremely optional AA meetings.

They stepped out of the car and hugged briefly, then moved to their respective apartments. Kip said, "Sure you wouldn't spend the weekend with me? Play pool. Go bowling. Drink vodka. Wild and crazy sex. Whatever you want."

Marty glanced over her shoulder. "Eat your heart out, big boy. I love you." She slammed her door after she blew him a kiss.

Kip screened an ancient Bob Hope movie. Startled by the phone ringing, he awoke from a dream of Dorothy Lamour in a sarong. He grabbed the phone and mumbled, "Yeah."

A voice said, "There's an emergency. Go to the encrypted element on your laptop."

He did it, stumbling in the dark, still groggy and a bit dazed. He fired up the laptop first. A red light and then a bell. "Tony, Rocco and wives killed. Maybe a mob hit. Get to work and see what you can find out."

"Oh, shit. Oh, shit. Damn it. Shit!" He dialed Marty's cell.

"Hey, I'm at the airport," she said. "We've already said good-bye."

"Big emergency. Can't leave. Tony and Rocco and wives killed." He turned on a lamp near the phone.

"I'm fed up with this shit. Why the hell did you do this to me?"

"Hah! Hah! Pick you up at the Northwest gate in twenty." They had secrets. He knew she'd cry but not show him. He didn't let her know how he hated the killing and violence and suffering.

The four murders generated a two-column heading and story in the Dallas Morning News. Mysterious deaths of retired businessmen from the East and their wives, shot to death in a downtown condo. Local police reported no suspects, and no persons of interest in the case. A local blogger said, "Who the hell would kill volunteers from the Landing? They helped the homeless find a better life. It's beyond belief."

Police searched for a motive, but there were no threats from Kitty Kat customers or romantic relationships from there that had soured. The manager suggested that both Teri and Maryanne had been outstanding employees, who won the admiration of customers, band members, and other entertainers and workers at the club. "In different ways," he said.

The investigation, covertly by the FBI, widened into the subterranean world of mafia politics in New York and New Jersey. No evidence of a breach in WPP secrecy could be substantiated. No warnings, threats, or intimidation by former gangland associates were discovered. Fifty interviews by trained FBI interrogators fell flat. Most importantly, no "contract" had been issued on the life of either Rocco or Tony.

The second day after the murders, Kip and Marty endured a speakerphone conference call with Reg, recently promoted to FBI Regional Chief. He referred to them as Sluggo and Nancy, out of a sense of secrecy rather than disrespect, but it annoyed them. He was still mystified by an FBI security breach, though it happened frequently. It just couldn't be random or coincidence, or could it?

Kip said, "All my witness people were pretty good. A couple of strays but back in line quickly."

Reg said, "I'm not blaming you two. Just strange. I don't know if we'll solve it."

Marty roamed Kip's living room, performing Zumba movements and then shadow boxing.

"We were certain that it was retribution. Mafia getting even. The Bureau has thrown everything we have into it. Crime lab worked 'round the clock."

Marty said, "Crime-scene forensics show anything?"

"Not really," Reg said. "Some fibers and threads. A lot of prints on the table, no blood spatter that's unusual. Somebody just shot these four people in the head. No self-defense or fighting back, so it could have been a friend or a neighbor or some mobster that they trusted. Nothing stolen and no forced entry. No witnesses. Must be a whack job, a hit man quickly in and out of town."

Kip said, "They wanted out." He plopped down on the couch.

Reg said, "Why the hell didn't you tell me? Maybe there's some kind of clue or motive there."

Kip said, "It's in my final report."

"You dumb shit. Always call me right away if something like that comes up. I'm sorry."

"It's okay. I told them both that we had them by the short hairs, digital recordings and so on. They calmed down." Kip gave a thumbs up to Marty.

Reg said, "Christ, you didn't threaten them, I hope."

"Yes, I guess I did. I don't see how that got the four of them shot to death." His stomach growled with tension, the past screwing up the present.

Reg said, "Maybe, just maybe, they reacted to your threats by reaching out for help from their old friends. You said they wanted out."

Marty stopped moving. "Any evidence that they contacted mob guys?"

"No, none at all. No phone calls, trysts, messages. Nothing."

Marty flipped the bird to the phone. She curtsied and ended her dance routine.

Kip said, "I don't think they'd reach out. Not enough time has gone by yet."

Reg said, "Probably right, Kip. I'm barking up the wrong tree. Maybe they tried to sell something to raise some money." The accusing tremor in his voice diminished.

Marty said, "Any evidence of that? Jewelry? Cash? Wire transfers? Drugs? Stock certificates?" She lay back on the couch, now relaxed and comfortable, pleased with herself.

"No," Reg said. "And we didn't find any evidence of a plan to leave. No tickets. No reservations. No house purchased in Mexico or the Caribbean."

Kip said, "I hope we're on the same page. That you still trust us." He pressed his palms together prayerfully.

Marty turned her body toward Kip. "Please trust us, Reg."

"Oh, of course, I have so much faith in our Sluggo and Nancy that I want you both to see if you can dig up anything at the Landing. Any clues on the murders. ASAP."

Marty said, "Now?" She rolled off of the couch and jumped up.

Reg coughed. "Yesterday. With Rocco and Tony dead, no one there knows who you really are except Dock. Those three that Kip mentored as a volunteer think you're now street people. Down on your luck. Keep your eyes and ears open. Be careful. Report directly to me. We've got even more than theft or drug-deal rumors about Dock. Get me that fucking killer. Nobody at that center will tell the cops or FBI shit. Too scared. They've got plenty to hide without snitching."

Kip said, "We're on it." He hugged Marty.

Reg coughed again. "They were killers and mobsters, so I don't feel too bad about them. But it makes the FBI look bad, like we can't protect our own witnesses. Happens too goddamn often."

Marty grimaced. "At least we can avenge their deaths." Conference call concluded, she sat down on the sofa and poured two glasses of vodka. She handed one to Kip. "Sluggo and Nancy toast Reg." They gulped them Russian style, no ice cubes or olives; but no black bread or beets or radishes or smoked fish, either.

Kip said, "Take a breather. We'll rest a bit. Dock will be interviewed downtown by the FBI today. We can just walk in like we own the place."

After a pot of coffee, Kip and Marty headed straight for Dock's office. The nameplate on the door simply said "Director." They knocked and strolled in confidently, as if the director had said, "Come in and sit down."

Marty said, "This will be damn hard to explain to Dock, if he finds out, but the stakes are very big. Four people dead." She peered at the framed licenses and certificates hung neatly on the wall.

Kip said, "You take the desk. I'll look in the files. Look underneath the drawers and see if anything is taped, like a picture or an FBI wanted poster or a newspaper story."

Marty reached in the bottom drawer and pulled out a piece of paper containing a handwritten poem. "Voilà!" She read it to Kip:

RATS

Rats leave a sinking ship,
Prefer to go elsewhere on a trip.
Rats don't really care about others,
They only want to have their druthers.
Rats escape prison to be protected,
Evade responsibility so not detected.
Rats deny their own bad behavior,
They snitch and lie about a superior.

Kip said, "The SOB isn't too careful about what he says or where he leaves it. Put it back. He sure hates rats. Probably has good reasons. Tony and Rocco were rats."

"You know, I was thinking to myself that it's kind of unusual for a guy with a PhD to be a director of the place," Marty said. "He's pretty slick."

"Is he a thug? Been in the can?" Kip ruffled the files, searching for something of interest.

Marty opened and closed drawers. She slammed the last one shut. "Nothing else here. His background check was clean. Financial, educational, professional, and job history. And all that."

"Computers fuck up. We know that. They might have stopped with a Texas criminal history, but not the national FBI database." He selected several files to study.

Marty sighed and raised herself up from a crouch. "Must be more to Dock?"

Kip said, "Here's gold. A file marked 'Financial' has a nice surprise, a ticket from EZ Money Pawn Shop, number 210."

A knock came on the door followed by a timid voice. "Who's there? Is that you, Doctor?"

Marty said, "It's us. Marty and Kip. Dock asked us to clean up his office."

"Oh, okay. It's usually a mess."

"I'm on my horse. Saddle up, boss." Marty said. She hurried out the door and directly to their car.

Kip followed. "Stay calm, Tonto. Okay, I'm in the saddle." The old car engine rumbled and finally fired up. "Hi, Ho, Silver. Away."

Marty said, "He's awfully naïve. Stupidly trusting SOB."

They drove straight to the motel address on the pawn ticket. A dusty, swirling wind barreled through the open car windows, drying the sweat from their skin before beads could form. The air conditioning seldom worked and, when it did, it gave off a disgusting odor of dead fish. The "off" button remained stuck.

Kip looked at Marty, who dozed during the ride, unsure of at what point her consciousness and sleep merged. Not talking, he couldn't keep his mind from the homeless. Cows had barns, chickens lived in coops, birds built nests, dogs slept in their master's bed, so why did the homeless turn to a grubby, urban, landscape without roots. No home, apartment, or igloo. Nothing attached to the land, only a tent or box or sleeping bag or blanket-roll. Home-lessness rivaled the plight of those caught up in the globe's worst natural disasters, except the latter generally got better emergency medical care. As Kip braked to avoid a skunk in the road, Marty awakened with a job to do.

The wind died down. Pawn number in hand, Kip's hopes mir-rored the bright sun and blue skies. An arrow on the Hi-Ho Motel sign, battered by the sins of time, pointed their car to the office at the far end of the nondescript twelve-unit rectangular build-ing. Beneath the peeling white paint on the door, several words could barely be deciphered, "Come on in" and "Pawn here." The near-death vertical slide of the Hi-Ho stopped with pawn. From new motel with daily charges, to old motel with weekly rates, to monthly flophouse, to prostitutes, drugs, and crime, and then to pawn. A new interstate highway that bypassed an old state road re-routed most traffic away from the Hi-Ho.

Marty scanned the seedy remains. "Definitely a neighborhood in decline. Could be temporary housing for the homeless. They could send a van out here to take people to their jobs or medical appointments, even bring them in for meals at the Landing. Have social services here too. Twelve rooms with two per room."

Kip nodded. "Better stay with our current job." They entered and he pushed the bell on the desk. Missing its ringer, no sound emerged. "Hello. Hello. We need pawn number 210."

"Maybe management is out to lunch." She poked Kip in the ribs. "Laugh, asshole."

"Come on out, wherever you are," Kip said.

"Hold your horses, folks. I'm just zipping up. Been in the crap-per." Buster stumbled out, wiping his mouth with his sleeve, small maroon spots dotting the front of his dirty white T-shirt. "Yep, surprise, it's me, Buster. Part-time job. A room now and then and a meal here and there. They are hard-up here." He chuckled and coughed. "Going to shack up? Got hourly rates. Seen you around the Landing."

Kip said, "We've seen you, too. We need your help, Buster. I'm Kip and this is Marty. We need pawn number 210. Lost the ticket."

Buster thumbed through an ancient ledger. "Yessirree. Small detective's gun. $200."

Marty said, "Is it here? Can we see it?" She leaned her breasts on the counter across from Buster, fluttered her eyelids, and licked her lips flirtatiously.

"Nope. Boss don't keep stuff here. Ain't safe."

Marty said, "You need the ticket to get the gun, right. If it's not redeemed, the boss can sell it."

"I think so," Buster said. "Something like that. A body gets powerful thirsty out here. Have any wine?"

Kip said, "Next time, Buster. We'll save up the $200, so we can buy the gun soon." They shook hands.

"Okay, folks, whatever you say. I like chocolate, too." He made a sucking sound.

"How do you get back and forth to the center?" Marty asked. "Need a ride?"

He shook his head. A dirty Mavs' baseball cap slid off. "No, Dock takes me in the van."

As they walked out, Kip said, "Let's lift Dock's prints from a glass or a fork or a pen from his desk or something, and get them to the FBI Crime Database. Reg will do it ASAP. Then they can get a search warrant to get the gun, the hate poem, and the pawn ticket, and who knows what other stuff. Doesn't protect his backside."

Marty said, "I've got a belly-full of this shit, these crooks and killers. Some days I'd just like to be a full-time mother or really help someone. Reminds me of that Mexican truck driver I married as a kid. He was one SOB. Jealous and bossy, he beat the shit out of me at least once a month. My mother told me in Spanish to stay, that's the way it is. I left him and made sure he never found me." She slammed the car door.

Kip turned to her. "I need a shower. Very hot and very strong. Join me? Could be fun. Can't get that at the Landing, but we can always sit outside for a long time in a warm rain. I can feel my scar and my eye twitches like crazy. I'm positive Dock's our perp, a real asshole."

Chapter Eleven

Kip and Marty choked down re-heated pizza for lunch, at home but dressed as homeless, ready for an afternoon at the Landing.

Marty said, "It's a lead-pipe cinch. I feel smug and self-satisfied and all that kind of shit."

Kip answered his cell. "Yes. Yes. Yes."

Marty raised her eyebrows. "So? Fingerprints work out?"

"We were so right. He's a felon, did a three year stretch at a New York prison, then violated parole and disappeared. It's our own Dock. The guy at the Bureau said that the prison records and the FBI database information were intact, but that he couldn't locate trial transcript files and probation officer's reports." Kip stood erect and flexed his muscles like a heavy-lifter. Adrenaline rushed through him as if he were twenty.

Marty said, "Probably his lawyer bought off a couple of IT clerks."

"And they're going to do the search warrants. The gun cooks his goose." He lay on the floor and crunched his abs with sit-ups.

"Did you forget the condo?" Marty said.

"I did, but the guys in Regional didn't. They went over the crime scene again. His hair, prints, and fibers put him there. Fibers from the carpet in his apartment were all over the floor. Bullet fragments should match the gun that killed them. Hoorah!" He stalked the room like a caged lion. Then he roared. Loud and long.

Marty said, "Let's celebrate. Put on our clean civvies, get out of these smelly costumes and have some vodka and burgers."

"Yes. Yes. Shit, let's just go like we are."

They hopped into their "job" sedan and headed for Arnie's for fun and relaxation. Kip's cell again. "Right. We never removed anything from his office or the pawn shop. Didn't mess with the evidence. Don't forget, I was a damn good, damn tough cop."

Several vodkas, burgers, and fries followed, and then several more vodkas.

"I should call Bill, right this minute," Kip said.

Marty said, "You should, but I have a different issue. Why don't you start to date? Your wife's been gone at least three years. It's time." She lowered her eyes, deflecting Kip's gaze.

Kip nodded. "I really want you. You know I love you. I fathered Roberto for you. Leave the professor. I love you." His lips were rubbery and wet.

"If I were twins, I would. I love Barbara. She's my life." Her head bobbed but her voice was clear.

"I better join a dating network for ex-cops."

Marty smiled at her success. "Hurrah. You're the greatest. She's lucky and she doesn't even know it yet."

They drove back to their apartments. Very slowly, to sleep it off.

Early evening, Kip's buddy at the Bureau woke him up on his landline. Though groggy, the news stirred up an instant flood of brain activity. "No shit. That can't be. Maybe Buster told him about the gun itself, but the pawn ticket and poem should still be there. It's only been a day. Goddammit!" He slammed the phone into the cradle.

Kip calmed down before he called Marty's cell. "You won't believe this. They found forged documents, but no gun, no ticket, no poem. His clothing fiber is also at the condo, but he could have been there on other occasions. Can't match the bullets or fragments to the gun, if there's no weapon. No shell casings, either. Murphy's Law in spades." Still stunned by the news, Kip stumbled around the room like a wounded deer.

Marty said, "We'll get him on parole violation, several possible thefts, maybe conspiracy to deal drugs. Go back to sleep, boss. We'll win this somehow. Here's a kiss for you."

Kip said, "Kiss back at you. The dumb schmuck let the gun be so easy to find, but he's a quick study. Removed the evidence. His prison background and the felony conviction still look bad for Rod Mulligan, aka Dr. Ralph Meade, aka Dock."

Early the next morning, Kip, freshly shaven and cologned, pulled on black slacks and a white open-necked shirt. He knocked on Marty's door, found her in yellow, fashionably updated clam diggers and a blue tank top. "Great minds. No need for undercover disguises. No need to play homeless. Somebody told him about our office visit and the EZ Pawn. Let's have a good breakfast and make plans."

"You took the words out of my mouth. Eggs ranchero for me. I know just the place. You can have grits, eggs, and sausage gringo. You'll love it."

Marty knew her stuff. At the Blue Cactus, strong coffee and spicy food stirred the blood although Kip wanted a Bloody Mary. Or two. "There's not enough to arrest him and charge him with murder. He is a parole violator and that could send him back to jail. Let's go see him for just an informal chit-chat, nothing for the courtroom."

Marty said, "Flip you for the bill. Heads."

Kip threw a quarter into the air. He caught the spinning coin and turned it over on top of his left hand. "Tails. Better luck with Dock."

Marty lifted both hands to eye level. "I want to have my nails done before we go back to that place."

An hour later they were in the old sedan again headed for Dock. "Feel better?"

She flashed her long red nails. "Much," she said. "My toenails are also out of control. I'll have my hair done tomorrow. Beginning to be me again."

"I'll bet a lot of homeless folks feel so dirty, covered with so much crud and grime, that the tiny pieces of soap in the Landing's showers don't do the job."

Marty said, "A spa experience would suit many. Some probably prefer the dirt, sweat, old clothes, messiness, craziness, and poor health. They either get used to it, or want to hide out, maybe they feel they deserve it. Who knows?"

Once at the Landing, they trailed Dock as he methodically limped around the outdoor plaza, supervising the clean-up. After a night packed with homeless in sleeping bags, the deposits of half-eaten candy bars, beer cans, wine bottles, pieces of human excrement and torn, dirty clothing were loaded for the dump.

Next, soaping and hosing down of the whole plaza and finally an application of a strong disinfectant. It still stunk to high heaven.

"We need more toilet facilities," Dock said. "You two look rejuvenated. End of undercover, I presume?"

"Thanks," Marty said. "Can we talk somewhere else? This mess is …" She held her nose.

"Sure." Dock led the way to the inside men's sleeping area. Simple metal cots covered with thin mattresses and old army blankets begged for the clean-up crew, so the aroma hardly improved. Dock kicked away a pile of moist, used condoms. "Men with men or men with women? Who knows?"

As they hurriedly entered the hallway, Kip said, "Dock, you know the saying 'get them by the balls and their hearts and minds will follow'? Famous during the Vietnam War. That's where we've got you."

"Do you now? That's interesting. How so?" He leaned on his good leg after he stopped in his tracks, hitched up his trousers, and pursed his lips in a nasty smirk.

Marty said, "We know from the FBI database that you're a convicted felon who spent three years in a federal cell, then skipped out on parole and came here."

"Is that all?" He limped on, hiding his face from them.

Kip said, "Not really. You're a clever fellow. We want the gun and that pawn ticket, even that poem you wrote. You're a goddamn thief and worse, a cold-blooded killer."

Dock said, "Why would a gun be important to you?"

Marty said, "We believe that your gun killed the two couples at Rocco's condo."

"That's crazy. Both were good guys who helped out a lot here. We depend on our volunteers. I knew their wives, too. Very fine folks giving back to their community."

"Bullshit," Marty said. She pulled on her earrings and twirled them.

"What about their background?" Kip asked. "You must have suspected something."

Dock said, "They were clean. No criminal, no foreclosure or bankruptcies. Both retired businessmen from out East." He moved on.

Marty said, "Anything out of the ordinary? Drugs, booze, jail, and so on?"

"Not a thing," Dock said. "They were a great asset here. Tony cooked and Rocco helped out with the food wagon at night and social services during the day."

Dock limped ahead a few paces, then turned to face them, trembling and sweating. "As my homeless folks would say, you're both full of shit. I do good work here, God's work if the truth were told. I have a PhD and a solid work history of helping others. Why not let it alone? Maybe I made a mistake years ago but I paid the price for it."

Kip said, "No can do, Dock. No way. You're a convicted felon and now you've killed four more people. The men were two of your best and brightest."

Marty said, "We know you've done a decent job here, except for the lack of housing, but you can't skip on this stuff. Four dead human beings."

Dock walked on ahead, trying to ignore his limp. "You can't use anything I say here in court. You haven't arrested me or detained me. You haven't read me my Miranda rights. You can't. You're not really FBI agents, you just work on contracts, not even cops anymore. I haven't been charged with anything."

Kip said, "We're just chatting but you're obviously a person of interest. We hear that you will be arrested and charged soon. Tell us what happened. Maybe you've got a good defense."

"I do. Let's pretend. Hypothetically, let's say we were planning a big drug deal. My partners said they'd report me to the Feds." Dock now stood his ground.

"So you defended your freedom?" Marty said. She ran her fingers through the bangles hanging from her ears.

"Exactly," Dock said. "They could have put me back in prison. I could have reported them to the mob and gotten them killed that way. A trade-off."

Kip said, "So you took matters into your own hands?" The long scar from ear to throat turned hot and thick.

Marty said, "Where's the gun? They've got your clothing fibers at the condo. Your prints, too. You're finished, Dock. Cooperation will save us all a lot of time and money."

"Let's be honest. I have been at Rocco's apartment a few times in the past. But you don't have a confession, a murder weapon, an eyewitness, or a very realistic motive, so you can't connect me or any gun, for that matter, to the bullets that killed them. You just suspect me. I did my time in prison. That doesn't mean I'm a cold-blooded killer. I was at my apartment the evening of the murders. Listened to a radio run by my generator for half an hour. Fell asleep on the couch." He walked into his office and slammed the door. He yelled, "Did anyone see me? Bring me an eyewitness to place me at the crime scene, even near it!"

Kip yelled too. "You're right! Our lawyers probably can't prove it beyond a reasonable doubt. Shit, you did it."

They moved through the hall, across the plaza, and to the parking lot.

Marty nodded. "Where would he hide the ticket and the gun? What would you do?" They reached their car and opened the doors. "I'd burn the poem and the ticket. The gun is a different story."

"The pawn-shop guy could testify about the gun, same model that killed the four of them. Circumstantial. We need the gun, itself," Kip said. The scar felt like it would jump off of his face. "And Buster, well, he wouldn't be a very credible witness, even sober. Supposedly, he told the FBI that Dock planned to have dinner at Rocco's condo. Our system protects…"

"Murderers," said Marty. "I need a drink."

Lady Luck blessed them the next morning. Kip's cell buzzed. "No shit. You found a drop of blood and a microscopic fragment of skin on one of Dock's shirts. The DNA and blood type match Tony. That's what I'm talking about. Give us until noon before you move in." He hummed the national anthem while he found clean clothes.

Kip pounded on Marty's door. "Get dressed. Hurry. We got a big break."

They rushed to the Landing and found Dock at breakfast, coffee with biscuits and gravy and a tiny, half-spoiled orange. "Sit down, please. Join me. I hoped you'd gone on to greener pastures."

Kip said, "You're fucked. They found Tony's blood on one of your shirts. You're going to need a damn good lawyer. They're going to arrest you."

He pushed his chair away from the table. "You two ruin my appetite. Tony cut himself in the kitchen all the time. I was there with him plenty. You know that. You're behaving like dogs with a bone."

Marty smoothed her hair and rubbed her eyes. "You fucking liar."

Kip bolted upright, grabbed him by the collar, and forced him back to the table. "She's right."

Dock's hands shook and beads of sweat poured down his forehead from neatly combed blonde hair. "I like to compromise, to negotiate. You know what I'm saying?"

Kip said, "What's your offer?" He released his hold on Dock.

Dock squirmed. He looked around the room. "I knew a Mafia chieftain in prison. We traded secrets. He told me about numerous 'hits,' but he was only convicted for extortion and bribery and got five to ten years. He's probably out now."

Marty said, "You'd be a snitch? You'd testify in court or give a deposition under oath?" She shrugged in disbelief.

Dock smirked as he blinked his baby-blues several times. "Yes, and I've got a damn good memory. Couldn't have gotten my doctorate without it. Some digital recordings, pulled them out last night in case you pinned me down. My rich, powerful attorney somehow obtained copies of a few recordings of phone conversations and discussions inside the federal prison. Here's an example on my digital recorder." He pressed the "play" button.

Meade: Call me Rod. I'm your new cellmate.
Ben: I'm Benedetto. Call me Ben. They say I stole stuff and ran a gang. Crapola.

Meade: They say I shot some guy during a robbery. I'm a thief not a killer.

Ben: How long? I think I can get parole in five, had a good lawyer.

Meade: Me, too.

Ben: What will you do?

Meade: I don't know. Maybe leave the country. Maybe go to school. You?

Ben: I should kill the judge. He was out to get me.

Meade: I got ratted out. By my buddy who told me I'd only drive the getaway car. He lied to save himself. He got stabbed in prison.

Ben: Nobody's got no principles. No honor. Save yourself, no matter what. The hell with the next guy.

Meade: You're right. I think I'll help other people. It's a great way to hide-out and do what you want.

Ben: I got some good bed time stories for you when we get to know each other better.

"See, our cell covered the end of the block. A window looked out on the courtyard, but the bars let us peek at the guards. I remember that grease-ball Sergeant Riley, stationed near the stairwell. They all knew Benedetto and profited from it. Candy, cigarettes, booze, perfume, cash, food, tickets to rock concerts or sports events. Whatever the prevailing medium of exchange at the moment.

"Bedtime, lights out, grew into a special story-time, a mutual confession for us. My tiny peccadilloes' contrasted with Benedetto's contract hits, large-scale heists, big-time extortion and prostitution rings. We foolishly trusted each other. Very foolishly as it turned out for charming, sweet, old Ben. He even served red wine and Italian string cheese during story-time."

Kip said, "All of this would have to be checked out. Make sure your story matches the situation. What would you want, assuming you were this valuable to the Bureau?" His eye twitched mercilessly.

"Forget the past. Immunity for the other stuff. So two hoods got themselves whacked. So what?"

Marty said, "And the wives? What about them?"

"Unfortunate that it went that way. Mob wives aren't worth much. But Benedetto Martinelli is the head of the biggest crime family in south Florida. That's the trade."

"You bastard," Marty said. "You've got plenty of reason to lie to save your ass."

Dock's face turned blank, mask-like. He froze in place. His hollow voice echoed. "Here's my real problem. It wears me out to be someone else, to use up so much energy to hide the truth. It's hurtful to hide crimes and needs, to always be ready to carve out a new identity."

Kip said, "I'll report all this to the Bureau's Regional top dog. He'll contact Justice in Washington. You'll be arrested around noon. Don't say anything, even after you get a lawyer. Stay silent for now."

As they walked to the car Marty said, "Tony cut himself, my ass. He's a liar and a murderer."

"Maybe," Kip said, "just maybe, his testimony to rat out the mobster will be worth it. Maybe parole violation for him with a year or two back in the pen. We'll see. I'd like to beat the truth out of him, but I won't."

Benedetto Martinelli was indeed big time, very big time. The Bureau flew Dock to Manhattan for interrogation and lie-detector tests. His information and pledge to give it under oath at a secret deposition and a trial played a critical role in reviving two cold murder-for-hire cases against Martinelli. Plenty of evidence to support his claims turned up.

The Don and Dock told tales of crime, bragged about violence, and naively trusted each other over meals and in the yard during exercise over a period of three years. Dock knew who, where, when, how, and the accomplices involved in the brutal, gangland killing of two local constables in upstate New York. They bled the mob for more payoffs after hijacking truckloads of untaxed cigarettes from Canada.

That night Kip dreamed about Dock. He visualized him on the

executioner's table, strapped in and ready to be injected. At the very last moment, a priest stormed into the room with the warden and said, "He's been saved. Last-minute reprieve."

Dock lay stone-faced while the priest sobbed and the warden said, "Next time, my friend. Next time."

Kip knew there would be a next time, but not in a prison.

Chapter Twelve

Kip fortified himself while he geared up for a long overdue, thorough cleaning of his apartment. He had been around the Landing long enough to recognize the gruff voice on his cell phone. It belonged to no one but Curtis L. Grund, CEO of a nearly bankrupt plastics firm, whose eldest son had died of a meth overdose while living on the street.

Mr. Grund, chairman of the Landing's Board of Directors, said, "You've done one helluva job, you and the FBI and the police and all of you. We missed a big one. Dock shocked us. Congratulations, young man."

Kip said, "Thank you, sir. Just doing our job." He stirred the ice and olive in his drink, then nibbled at a chip loaded with guacamole.

"We owe you one," Grund said.

"I'd like to explain something," Kip said. "Dr. Meade, Dock, is involved in some sensitive litigation on the east coast. Left here suddenly." He changed hands with his cell and poured more vodka over the ice.

Grund said, "I know. Fooled us pretty good."

"Yes, sir. He fooled a lot of people." He sipped the vodka slowly.

"We like your style, Kip. You're thorough and competent. You've got your finger on the pulse of the Landing and its people."

Grund's irritating, hacking cough forced Kip to momentarily pull the cell away. "Marty, my partner, deserves a lot of the credit."

"Well, we'd like you to interview to be Director for a year or two. Get the place on an even keel again. Take a leave from your contract position with the Bureau. I've checked on that already." Grund blew his nose twice and coughed again.

111

"I'm stunned," Kip said. "I had no idea. I like it. I've developed a real interest in the Landing." His heart pounded and he shook with excitement. He set his glass on the table.

"You'll make a lot more money than the FBI contract pays you. A free hand to straighten out the place." He stopped talking while he wheezed. "Better employee and volunteer background checks. Keep out weapons. We'll serve a lot more people if the economy gets worse. A lot more."

Kip said, "I should take some time to think it over. Evaluate a career change. Salary. Retirement and all that."

"Oh. I'm an old man. I'd better sit down. Maybe I need my oxygen tank."

"There are things I'd want," Kip said. He sucked on ice from his drink.

"Yes. Go ahead, I'm comfortable now." Kip marched proudly around his apartment, avoiding the litter of bottles, clothes, shoes and newspapers, pumped up by the excitement of the job possibility and the vodka. "It's very important to me. Dock did some good things, but I'd need more resources to buy or rent, and then rehabilitate, transitional and permanent supportive housing. Many abandoned buildings and apartments surround the Landing."

"I couldn't agree more. Dr. Meade thought the city or county or feds should take care of housing. The Board will be behind you. Neighbors won't like it at all. We'll need new ways to approach the community."

Kip said, "If the job is mine, I'll want that commitment from every member of the Board, even someone who doesn't want me."

"You're right." No uncertainty in Grund's voice or words. He was a straight-shooter. "The winds of hope, however hot and dry, must blow into the Landing. Please forgive me, it's almost time for my medication and afternoon nap."

Kip said, "My feeling is to do the best for the folks while we're here with them. Maybe a miracle comes along?" Kip dove onto the couch, overwhelmed by the interest and strong support.

Grund said, "That's a yes for the interview tomorrow? My cell is nearly gone. Anything else?"

"We need something fun for these suffering folks." He straightened up, his face flush with creative excitement.

"Okay. Okay. Sounds good. The Board will grill the hell out of you. Your background…"

"I won't stay forever. Maybe a year or two. Probably go back to being a PI or the Bureau's witness program. Thank you, sir. I'm very grateful for your support and the opportunity for an interview."

Kip took some time to get ready for the interview. He felt lucky, so he shopped and spoiled himself. He spent too much money on a professional barber, trimmed his beard with short sideburns and level buzz-cut. Next, he bought dark slacks and a grey silk shirt for the interview. He decided against a suit and tie, he was now one of the people, not necessarily the unwashed, but definitely not one of the elite Board.

The next morning at 11:00 a.m., Mr. Grund ushered him into the Board meeting room.

"Come in, Kip. Nice to see you. Please take a seat. Kip, the Board has six business and professional members. Ms. Abby Ringold, next to me, a prominent attorney, is vice-chairperson. Mr. Ahmad Saleh, a well-known businessman, is the secretary-treasurer. He's sitting at the end."

Saleh smiled and said, "We don't want to throw good money after bad. Must be very cautious."

Kip observed that their designer-furnished conference room flaunted genuine wood paneling and several velvet curtained windows, now wide open to the courtyard. A gentle breeze assisted the over-worked air conditioning system, so much so that the men kept their suit coats on and the women placed shawls or sweaters around their shoulders. The drop in temperature mirrored the Board's cool smiles and nods as he sat.

Abby said, "Curtis, I'm going to reset the A/C. I'm downright cold." She walked to the wall thermostat and adjusted it. "It's sweaty hot everywhere else in the Landing."

Abby fluffed her short, blonde, curly doo with both hands. She was a show-off, appearing unduly perky and spirited in her early fifties. Multiple Botox injections every few months to keep the dream alive. She took over. "Kip, could you give us your full name and…"

Grund said, "I'll start. Everyone, this is Kendrick Crandall, known to us as Kip. That okay, Kip?"

Like a huge bongo drum, several Board members beat their fingers on the table. Another poured coffee. One sneezed. Abby, shivering perceptibly, adjusted the A/C again.

"Kip," Grund said, "you'd be an unusual choice to be Director, to say the least. No social work or psychology degree. Not much management experience. Tell us why you're right for the job." He slouched in his armchair as his lids fluttered and tried to close.

Kip smiled and said, "I'm your law-and-order candidate. Been a cop and an army MP, then worked several jobs on an independent contract with the FBI, Police Joint Task Force. We got Dock. He's gone. Of course, we can't undo the drug scheme we discovered or the four murders, or anything else. My approach would be to make sure we have better security for the Landing, serious background checks on staff and volunteers, and more accountability of the leadership to the homeless folks, the entire community and the Board."

Grund said, "Plenty of cops are crooks, too. Why don't you go back to being a PI or join the police force again? You did good work there."

Kip turned toward Grund. "I might later on. First, I want to improve things here. Go forward with the Landing."

Grund said, "Don't cops think in terms of black and white, just crime and punishment? Jail or prison or detention?" He sat up while his gaze moved to search out the approval of others.

"Yes, sir, we do. Just as we found out what Dock had done here and in the past, his crimes. He avoided the punishment he deserved for parole violation by becoming a rat, a snitch, on his cellmate in federal prison. It's a common thing in police work." His eye twitched, but only in one corner, and he felt his scar grow warm, not yet hot or thick.

Kip knew he'd be carefully vetted by the Board. He was prepared, but the Boy Scout motto didn't account for all the emotions that bubbled up during the third degree back and forth. His own doubts echoed the Board's in many ways. Was he right for the job? He didn't finish college. He had a functional drinking problem, under control while he worked, but who knew the future? Especially those weekends? He wasn't a social worker, or a traditional do-gooder, but he did believe in rules and order and security. And he liked what the Landing was trying to accomplish.

Abby asked, "Why in the world would you want to work with these losers? You believe in personal responsibility, don't you?" She closed her tablet and looked up with a self-satisfied smirk.

Kip squirmed in his chair and hesitated before he spoke. "Yes, I do. I believe the homeless have a responsibility to try to improve their lives. But we, the rest of us, also have a responsibility to provide services, a temporary home, and a measure of hope for their future."

Grund applauded awkwardly, his gnarled hands barely able to touch each other.

Kip said, "I developed an interest in several individuals while I volunteered here. Before any of the police or FBI work. Specifically, I mentored , or tried to, Tottie, Squeaky, and Namey. I wasn't an all-star. I did my best and that's what I'd do for everyone who comes through our door." The twitch disappeared and the long scar felt cool.

Grund said, "What about staff? Dock fooled us."

"That's an area I know very well. Background checks on all staff and volunteers. State and national databases, criminal, financial, past jobs. The works. Due diligence. And we'll carefully compare everyone with the FBI national criminal database, not just Dallas and Texas."

The entire Board nodded and applauded.

Grund said, "Exactly my sentiments. No guns or knives here. And no felons on the staff. Enough of that with our clients."

Kip went on. "If we work together, there are things I want..."

Abby said, "It's too warm for me now." After she went to the A/C again, a blast of cold air shot through the vents. She stood in front of the window fanning her face with her fingers turned inward. "Phew. That's better."

Kip said, "Please hear me out. I need your support to pursue both transitional and permanent supportive housing, not just raise millions over five years in a campaign for a new apartment building that takes months to build. We could use empty warehouse space, improve it with facilities and electricity, meet the minimum code for upgrades, so that fewer people spend the night in cardboard boxes or tents that leak. I want to provide provisional housing, that's my term for it. Then put some of our services right there in the housing."

Kip felt surprised when the buttoned-down Saleh in the fitted Italian suit spoke again. He had expected a cost-benefit analysis but heard an empathetic plea for expanded transitional housing, especially for the disabled homeless.

Saleh said, "Shelter with sheltered workshops expresses my attitude." He picked lint from his suit coat.

Grund said, "Yes, but keep the cost down. Way down, son."

"Also," Kip said, "I want to have monthly parties and social events for our people. Pizza and cakes and candy. Nothing fancy. Parties in the park or at the lake or a freebie in a hotel nearby. Fun things. These people need a few laughs and moments of pure fun. It won't cost that much, since we feed and clothe and house many of them already."

Grund said, "Right on." He grinned smugly at his own hip vernacular. "I should say right on, bro. You're our man. No vote needed."

Kip stood. "I don't have an exact budget but I could have one for the next Board meeting, if you select me."

"Anything else?" Grund covered his face with both hands while he coughed and hacked, then wiped them clumsily on a huge white handkerchief.

Abby said, "Curtis, may I have a few final words?"

"Go ahead." He anxiously shuffled some papers.

"Well," she said, "Kip, you must be very, very careful at the Landing. We must be very, very careful here on the Board. We don't want any more rumors of any kind of criminal or unethical behavior by staff or volunteers. Watch the place. Keep an eye on the staff. Even carefully selected people get into a new culture and do unusual things. Get my message. I'm voting against your appointment as the Director. I'm the only vote, it appears, against you. I might be the next chairperson." She shivered from the cold air, and pulled a sweater over her shoulders. "Let's go to lunch. My treat."

So Grund's chairmanship slid away from him, as other board members competed for leadership. He'd have to play ball soon with a new chairperson, but there was time to evaluate the possibilities, especially Abby.

Kip said, "Mr. Grund, I'll only take the job for a year or two. I want to make some new things happen. New ideas."

Chapter Thirteen

Kip screamed, jumped up and down, clapped, and shadow-boxed until he was breathless. He never felt this good as a cop. Oh, Marty. He'd have to tell her right away. He needed a drink.

He called her. "Meet me at Arnie's? Burgers and vodka."

Marty said, "Of course. Anything wrong?"

He bit this tongue. "I'll tell you there."

At Arnie's, the noise and cheering of pro sports on giant wall TVs drowned out other human communication. Kip found a booth with their favorite waitress. He winked twice and held up two fingers, code for two ice-cold vodkas with fancy blue-cheese olives and two burgers and fries deluxe.

Marty, hair askew and a drop of mascara dried on her cheeks, sat down. "Hi, sorry I took so long but my car stalled. Roberto has had the flu. I should be there. Sometimes I think I should be there all the time. You know, Ms. Mom."

"Would you like that?"

"I think I would for a while, just kick back and cook and clean and do laundry and take care of my kid and my wife." She tried to smile as she teared up.

"You're sick of the crooks and homeless. Want to relax. Try domesticity." He reached over the table and dabbed at her eyes gently with his handkerchief.

She tugged at her dangling gold and silver hoops. "That's it."

The drinks arrived. Kip touched his glass to Marty's. Then he leaned over and kissed her cheek. "To us. To our future. Sorry Bill, bless your heart."

Marty sipped. "So, what's the deal?"

"They want me to replace Dock for a while. I said yes." He put his glass on the table.

She stretched over the drinks and kissed Kip full on the lips. "I'll be damned. Congrats, boss. You're the best."

"I was worried about you. You were terrific. You can stay with the Bureau contract or re-open our PI business or be second in command at the Landing, work with me. Whatever you want."

Marty said, "Thanks. I hate the idea of us going different ways. Even for a while. I'm leaving."

"Of course I'll visit as much as I can. Roberto's my son, too." Kip swung at an imaginary pitch. "I'm a team player."

Hot tears now flooded Marty's face. She didn't try to wipe away the wet mascara. She gulped her drink. "You're always welcome. He has two mothers and one dad. We'll never lie to him." The burgers and fries arrived. "I need to learn to cook this stuff. And soon. My wife loves it."

"Your chile rellenos are fine with me. In fact, all I need is someone who looks like Beyoncé, sings like Whitney Houston did, and has your soul."

"At least you know what you want."

"My folks would have been so proud of our work together for the WPP and the Bureau. You know my black dad always teased my mom that he was part-this and part-that, and that made him stronger and better than any one-hundred-percent white woman. He was army all the way, and proud of it. It's no surprise that I decided to go to the police academy after some college and the army."

She smoothed her hair and used a tiny mirror to repair her makeup. "Didn't you want to help others? Change society? Make it a better place."

"You know, it sounds crazy, but I can't really remember. Seemed like a good idea at the time."

Abruptly, Marty arose and kissed him again. "Bye-bye. See you soon." She hurried outside.

He'd miss her terribly.

Kip stayed very busy, during the next few weeks. He tried hard and did a good job in his brief tenure as the Director of the Landing. The plan for the Community Meeting initiated his program to tamp down the fear or suspicion of the homeless living amidst a middle-class neighborhood. The concept of the Party-in-the-Park began a series of enjoyable, fun events for the Landing's residents. He theorized that the more such happenings occurred, the more likely that the chronically homeless would enjoy themselves, relax and have a good time. No silver bullet, just chipping away at their desperate, rigid lifestyle. He hoped that violence would not mark these homeless-related events.

He even located a cavernous abandoned warehouse two blocks from the Landing and the Board backed him up with a good faith offer to buy the building and rehab it for dorms, toilet facilities, and two offices for social workers and drug counselors. He was off to a fast start.

Several weeks after Marty returned to Detroit, Kip walked into the Landing's dining room. The sweetish aroma of food cooked in bulk dominated the humid room, not terribly unpleasant, though the sweaty steam-table section failed to be cooled by three huge fans.

Kip noticed her immediately. Long, straight black hair. Glints of silver in exotic almond-shaped dark eyes. Clear, light brown skin covering a slight, almost girlish figure.

He sauntered to her table where she was helping two young girls cut up the turkey sausage.

"Hi, I'm your new Director. Please call me Kip." He held out his hand.

She strained to stand up, but he motioned for her and the kids to stay seated. She shook his hand. "Nice to meet you. These are my twins. This is Kara and that's Karla. I'm Karen DeRoot from Seattle."

"Nice to meet you. Tough times?"

Karen said, "You better believe it. We came by bus nearly eight weeks ago. Your people found me a part-time job here. The girls will go to St. Anthony's down the street and we'll move into a half-way house. This place is a godsend." She sliced her own sausage into small bites.

"The girls are beautiful, simply beautiful."

Both girls, cheeks red, looked away with embarrassment.

"Thank you," Karen said. "Why don't you join us?" She motioned for him to use the fourth chair.

"Good idea. Be right back." He grabbed a tray and filled a plate with sausage, Cajun rice and green beans with hocks. As he returned to the table, he said, "Oops, forgot a fork."

Karen leaned over and handed him hers. "Spoon is fine for me."

"Thanks," Kip said. "Want to talk about it? You don't have to." He nibbled at the food.

"Yes, I've got no big secrets from the girls. They're seven and saw and heard most of it."

"On second thought," Kip said, "let's wait until later. I've got my story, too."

"Fine. This food tastes good." She took tiny bites. "We've gained weight here. When we travel, we usually have rice and fish or a Ramen noodle soup."

The girls nodded and giggled.

Karen ate slowly, savoring each mouthful. "We were very lucky. We're going to have the last bedroom at the half-way house for women and kids. Wonderful people. They've supplied everything for us."

Karla moved close to her mother so she could whisper in her ear.

Karen said, "The girls have to pee. We'll see you tomorrow."

"Until tomorrow, then. I want to see more of you. And the girls, of course," Kip said. "If there's anything I can do, just ask."

"We will." She touched his hand.

Kip headed for his office, tantalized by Karen, eager to know her, anxious to help and share her quiet resolve. His heart beat fast and his breathing needed some instant Yoga. "My God, could she be the one?" he whispered.

It had been a long time. Though Wendy had been gone for years, the loneliness and desperation of her cancer battle left Kip with scars of helplessness and loss that never seemed to heal. Wendy and his own mother shared the vulnerability of a woman open to feelings and emotions, still possessed of the strength required to cope with life. He sensed that Karen resembled them. At least, he hoped she did.

Kip's cell interrupted the reverie with some ugly rap music. Marty's voice, slow and tortured, cried into the phone, "A car ran over Roberto! It may be a concussion."

"Oh, no, please God, no." Despite a cop's training to handle stress, fear and panic raced through his body. His hands shook, nearly dropping the cell. That churning in his stomach took hold.

"Barbara and I are at the emergency room. I'll call with any news."

Kip said, "I'll fly up to Detroit if you need me."

He poured himself a triple vodka, added some ice cubes and cheap Spanish olives from his small office fridge, closed his eyes, and tried to piece together the last hour of his life. Wendy, his lost love, Marty, his former love, and Karen, his current infatuation, hit the pleasure-pain button in his mind, offset by the stunning news of Roberto's situation. He downed his drink, spit out an olive pit, and then dozed off for an hour or so, sitting upright at his desk. The land-line woke him with a start. "Yes, yes. Who is it?"

Marty's calm voice soothed his jangled nerves and untied the knot in his stomach. "The docs say he's out of the woods. X-rays and CT scan all say the same. No permanent damage. Love to you, Daddy."

"Thanks, I'm so relieved. Somebody's watching over us," Kip said. "Very emotional day. Love to you three."

He'd tell Marty next time they talked. "I'm going in a family direction. The father of a wonderful son. I've just met a lovely woman with twin daughters. I know what I want, what I've missed, a home and family."

Before he mobilized himself to go back to his apartment, a gentle knock came on the office door. "Hi, it's Karen. Anybody there?"

Kip flew to the door. "What a nice surprise. Come in."

"The girls were settled for the night, so I thought…"

"I'm glad you're here. I felt we had some kind of connection. It's been a roller coaster. My biological son was injured but he'll recover fully. So all is well. Please sit down." He eased a chair closer to his desk.

Karen said, "What happened?"

"I don't know details but he was hit by a car."

Karen said, "You're still married?" Her gaze floated aimlessly around the room.

"No, no. I'm the father of a young son to two moms. I lost my own wife to cancer." Kip switched on the desk lamp to bathe the office in a mellow glow. "Care for a drink?"

"Yes."

"Vodka or water? Not much of a choice."

"Just the water. I'm in recovery." Karen smiled briefly, her dark eyes shining with humility and pride. "You know, Kip, I've been virtually alone with the girls for more than a year, and on the run for weeks. Their dad is a very bad dude, does coke, can't hold a job, abuses us in many ways, but wouldn't let go. We left."

Kip gave her the water. "Lousy guy. You did the right thing. Divorce him?"

"Absolutely. Definitely. If I'd felt safe, it would have happened in Seattle. I'll find a way here."

"And the girls?"

"It's so hard on them." Karen cried as she shook her head. She put her hands to her face. "They still love him and miss him terribly. They saw and heard far too much with him. Scared them. They need a bedroom and their own desks and their own music. We'll get counseling. Believe me, homeless is no way to raise a family."

Kip stood and walked to Karen, placed his hand on her shoulder. "I wish I could ease some of the suffering."

Karen's hand covered his. "You have. Listening is helping."

"You know, I've been alone for a long time. I've had strong feelings for my ex-partner, Marty. We worked together night and day for several years. We'd both been cops and PIs before working in the FBI Witness Protection Program. We did some undercover stuff here and I ended up head of the Landing."

"Quite a bio," Karen said.

"My true commitment was my wife Wendy. Tried to help her and wipe away the pain, but the cancer conquered both of us and it took her. I drank and drank. I'm still working on it, sometimes more than others, but that's obvious."

Karen framed his face with her hands and kissed him longingly on the lips. They embraced. She whispered, "Romance pops up in the most surprising ways, doesn't it?" She opened the door before he could speak. "You need your own nest."

He said, "Wendy would definitely agree. I'm sure. So would my mother. Well, my father, too, he taught me to take care of those I care about. By the way, my father was black."

"Mine, too."

A jolt surged through him. Both had black fathers, in addition to the immediate personal connection that ignited the intense, needy feelings. He returned to his apartment, exhausted by the day, yet his racing mind prevented immediate sleep. He had to see her very soon, but he couldn't take his eye off of the ball.

Kip arranged a Community Meeting for one week later. Topic, homeless transitional housing. St. Anthony's aging red-brick school building, two stories with white molding chipped nearly beyond repair, hosted an unruly crowd inside and out on the night of the presentation. This hot issue drew both cheers and jeers from those attending. Several uniformed police provided security at the door as well as in the parking lot adjacent to the church and school.

Signs and placards, in large print or hand-painted, stood out, carried by "vets" in uniform or by the Landing folks, a reminder that twenty percent of homeless folks nationally are vets. Veterans' signs included "Please Treat Solders Decent," and "Vets Need a Home."

Opponents of homeless housing bandied about small banners such as "No Free Lunch (or Home)," and "Get a Life." Angry feelings behind these polarizing attitudes revealed themselves openly on the faces of the neighborhood group. Security guards removed a homeowner screaming, "Get the fuck out!"

On the sidelines, apart from the crowd, an old-timer from AA or NA urged the addicted to attend twelve-step meetings on a regular basis. He held a small, simple black cardboard sign with "12" painted in white acrylic.

Inside the hall, peeling, green, painted walls surrounded windows adorned with visions of the Holy Virgin and the baby Jesus, not the original stained glass, but restored with a plastic imitation.

"Advocates for the Homeless" seated themselves on one side of the room, counter-balanced by those representing a "Neighbor-hood Values." T-shirts crudely printed with these names left no doubt as to their predilections.

The chairperson spoke at a lectern connected to an ancient PA system, which still echoed in the rear of the hall. Buster, Queenie, Enuf-el and Namey sat in the homeless section, along with many others not so well-known to him.

Kip admired Karen and the girls, their attractive dresses laundered and pressed. Now settled comfortably into the halfway house, the twins had returned to school. Karen thought she had snagged a full-time job, and would go for a second interview for the secretarial position in a daycare center.

Kip's mind crazily wandered to booze, so he said a prayer instead of entering the chapel to sip sacred red wine. Bill would love that one.

The head of the neighborhood coalition, a thin woman simply dressed in black slacks and a blue button-down shirt, added a rainbow ribbon to her collar. "Please listen to me, I believe whole-heartedly in diversity. Diversity in schools, in jobs, in relationships, and of course, in housing. Our differences enrich our lives as we learn from and share the many ways in which we differ. But I'm also a realist. We've got plenty of diversity in our neighbor-hood already, gender, age, education, occupation, income, and so on. Homeless people, many through no fault of their own, maintain a lower standard of living, diminished expectations, and frequently engage in conduct such as lying, drinking, stealing, drugging, and other more serious crimes. Their behavior drags down a neighborhood like ours. Their values are simply too different, much too different from ours. Please understand, we want these people to have shelters, halfway houses, and, of course, eventually their own permanent apartments and homes. But, not here. Not now. Not ever."

Tumultuous applause greeted the talk, a few hoots of anger, and plenty of hollers of support, with repeated "Amens" and "We love you, sister."

The homeless and their advocates were nonplussed, mildly appreciative of the bold honesty expressed. Enuf-el said, "Man, she's something, ain't she?"

Karen arose, straightened her hem-line as she approached the lectern. A quivering hand held up the mike. "I'm Karen. My daughters attend school here and we live nearby in a halfway house. Were it not for the Landing and the halfway house, we'd be living on the street. I'm not here for compassion or to gain sympathy as a victim. We had a decent life in Seattle with my husband, who ran a warehouse while I worked in a childcare center. We paid our bills and, I thought, loved each other. I drank, but got into AA and stopped abruptly. Then he lost his job, and discovered coke and PCP. When drunk or high, he'd become insanely jealous, abusive, and he even threatened to kill us if I went to the police. So, finally the girls and I left with some money I'd saved, and the clothes on our backs. Would I be a bad neighbor? Would my values be so different from yours? What if my girls and I lived in transitional housing nearby? I'll have a full-time job soon. They're in school again. We've had our issues, but would we be too different from you and your families? Of course, you might think, 'She's fine but not the rest of them.' That's destructive, narrow-minded thinking. We're all God's children and deserve a chance here."

The homeless sat stunned, motionless and silent. Karen's talk had overwhelmed them, so emotional yet so realistic. Her words spun around, back and forth, to include them. Yes, there were some bad apples in their barrel, but that was always true. Karen spoke for them. They loved her.

Kip led Karen back to her seat. "That was wonderful, simply wonderful. I had no idea you were such a good speaker, so honest, so compelling. I'm very proud." He wanted to hold her and kiss her but didn't. The twins held hands, they smiled and pounded their feet with enthusiasm.

At last, the chairperson said, "We'll take a short break before the Q&A session. Thanks to both of our speakers. They've both made excellent presentations, but power is not always the same as fairness."

The twins remained seated while Kip and Karen scurried to a quiet side entrance. Alone, they kissed passionately. Lips, mouths, and tongues lost in time. Sirens in the background grew louder. Flashing lights signaled an EMS truck as it swerved into the parking lot. Many in the growing crowd of protestors and advocates, grim and strangely silent at first, began to sob as Kip and Karen approached.

Buster stumbled, eyes bleary and speech slurred. "Squeaky died in a fire."

That wasn't exactly what happened. Denty relayed the full story to Kip. "Squeaky, just about dead from AIDS and TB, was deliberately torched. They burned him to death in an oil drum full of blazing gasoline." This wounded warrior, who had two Purple Hearts and a Bronze Star, lived most of his life on the street. A favorite at many shelters he found a gory ending, one he surely didn't deserve. Denty fell to her knees in pain and prayer.

The first question on everyone's lips, including Kip, was "Why?" The second question, only the destitute would ask, was why didn't his killers leave his shoes, pants, shirt and hat for someone else. What a waste, just out to kill a homeless guy, but no concern for others without decent shoes and clothes.

"A selfish, fucking murder," Buster said.

Most of the crowd of about one hundred local and homeless people quietly dispersed as more police and a second EMT arrived on the scene, sirens blaring and lights flashing. Squeaky's burned body lay on the sidewalk after the overturned barrel spilled out his charred remains, still too hot to cover with a tarp. The crime scene was secured with tape and barriers, and authorities began the arduous task of reconstructing events and obtaining eyewitness accounts.

Kip, who thought he had seen it all as a cop, didn't really need this reminder that evil knew no bounds. It was not a pretty sight, a deliberate human barbecue, with that unmistakable horrifying smell of burned flesh. Rumors quickly spread through the by-standers that two skinheads with swastikas tattooed on their necks had done it. Someone speculated that Squeaky might have committed suicide, sick as he was, and that he feared the slow, painful AIDS-related death spiral.

"They hate us," Denty said. She now rocked on her heels near Kip and Karen. "We're scum. They don't want us here. They want us gone or dead."

Kip said, "Why kill Squeaky? He wasn't a leader or a spokesman for the homeless. He did congratulate me when I became Director."

"Nope. Just Squeaky, for better or worse. Just Squeaky. No family either." Denty attempted to cover his remains with her tattered shawl, but cops stopped her.

Karen's high-cheekboned face wrinkled with sadness as she held back tears. "What happens now?"

Denty slumped when Squeaky's remains were photographed by police. "Nothing. No one cares. They beat us up all the time. Either the cops or them vigilantes. They say we're not good Americans. Who wants to live out in nature and eat berries and wild roots? Shit."

Karen said, "And stop bothering all the good people in cities. They've got to learn to accept us as we are. We're all different."

"That's it. Don't dirty their streets." Denty grabbed her shawl and stomped on it. "I'm pissed off. Even those natives on beaches in Mexico braid hair, or sell bracelets, or hats or do fingernails and toenails for them tourists who pay a lot. Shit, we can't even do that kind of shit. Nobody would pay us. Big-time assholes. I call it bullshit."

Kip said, "They'll get whoever did this." His eye twitched.

Denty walked away slowly. "Bullshit. You're just one of us. Be careful out there." She stopped and carefully eyed Kip head-to-toe. "You're not half-bad. Want a good time? Not for free. I give good...

Karen pushed her hard toward the street. "Wrong guy. Wrong time. Wrong place."

Kip said, "I hope some veteran's group will raise money for a funeral. He was a vet. When the dust settles, we'll have a memorial service or dedication at the Landing. I'm a compassionate cop."

Karen wiped her eyes with a tissue. "Denty had it right. This killing is bullshit."

The remaining crowd, hushed into shock and still breathing the acrid stench of Squeaky's demise, oogled the death scene.

"Please step back, folks. Let us finish our work," a uniformed beat cop said. Police cruisers flashed their lights as did the EMT truck, but sirens were off.

Kip heard and watched the human aftermath of Squeaky's murder. Strangely quiet, no screams, few tears, just a stunned and empty group of homeless people. Typically they maintain some distance, a safe numbness, to life's ups and downs. Local TV crews interviewed a police captain nearby, but none of the homeless spoke on camera. Why bother? Photographers hurried to meet their deadlines, while the huge rain clouds snuffed out the man in the moon.

Kip said, "This murder might fuel stronger anti-homeless attitudes. He was so vulnerable. There won't be much public sympathy for this old man. Just some stinky plea deal for gang members or vigilantes." His facial scar heated up with angry frustration.

Karen tugged at Kip's arm. "Not our job today. We're after that Neighborhood Coalition. Remember? We've got the Homecoming Party soon." They edged away in silence, holding hands. The image of this cruel death engulfed them, while it somehow deepened their feelings for each other.

Chapter Fourteen

Two weeks later, free haircuts, shaves and trims, showers, slightly used fresh clothes, and a packet of comb, toothbrush and toothpaste signaled round one of the Landing's first Homecoming Party. Round two was a breakfast of muffins, bacon, sausage, grits, and fresh (not dried) eggs, finished off with steaming hot Jamaican Blue coffee, plenty of real cream and sugar, and a myriad of colorful donuts.

The line of unruly folks waiting to partake encircled the Landing, crowded the inside hallway, and maintained itself from 5:00 a.m. until 10:00 a.m. That knock-out response overwhelmed the showers, the staff, and the seating arrangements in the dining hall. "More soap!" yelled a staff member. "Grits are cold," called another. "Another pot of coffee," echoed throughout the kitchen. No referee could control the chaos.

The preliminaries succeeded well before the main bout began. Kip selected a patch of green, where some trees remained, crisscrossed between the aging semi-industrialized area and the skyscrapers of downtown. This small city park fit the bill for such a gathering, turning brown and increasingly treeless, a transitional setting, it was an ideal place as well as a natural symbol for the celebration.

Abby, the assertive Board member, told Kip that to honor the homeless, to gather them together like this, stirred up trouble for the area. Not the individual "troubles" of the homeless themselves, but incidents furthered by such a critical mass, theft, fighting, selling drugs, or worse. He ignored her warning even though he had a premonition that something horrible would happen.

Kip invited the neighbors. Few attended in person, though others mailed in contributions. He hoped, of course, for reconciliation based on a simple common-sense belief, when their neighbors and the homeless related to each other as individuals, as separate, real people, barriers slowly broke down. Then, and only then, would transitional housing projects face less opposition throughout the city. It just hadn't worked out that way. At least, not yet.

The tiny park wore festive balloons on bushes and the few small trees held red, white and blue flags, honoring the country and its people. A plea for respect, attention, and support.

Kara and Karla held Karen's hands as they approached Kip. He ran to them, close to the picnic tables already groaning with huge bowls of salads and vegetables, steaming vats of rice and potatoes. He nearly toppled the pungent meatloaf, ready to be sliced, as it sat firmly in large tin baking dishes.

The girls grabbed Kip's hands. When he leaned over to kiss Karen, the girls squeezed his fingers.

Kara said, "I want to have my face painted." Karla nodded.

Karen chuckled. "I've already done mine." She patted her purse.

They strolled to the table where kids held up their faces to a clown decorating them. She dressed as a gypsy. "Do you want to be an angel? How about a vampire?"

The girls looked up at Kip, then smiled at each other as they surveyed a poster board portraying visuals of these options.

Karen said, "Pick what you want. You don't have to be the same."

Karla whispered to Kara, who then said, "We'll both be vampires. We drink blood."

Kip wrapped his arms around Karen from behind, held tight, and bit her neck lightly. "I want to suck your blood."

Karen feigning fear, let her body tremble and turned as if to disengage. "Oh no, kind sir," she said, "anything but that." She kissed him hard. "You don't want to do that."

"Yes, I do."

Karen pulled away and stood ramrod stiff as she spoke. "There's another piece to my puzzle. Two years ago my husband made me HIV positive. I want you to know. I trust you completely."

"Oh, no!" Kip gulped down air in amazement, trying to catch his breath. "Hard to believe. The girls? What a bastard!" He touched the red hot scar on his cheek.

She held his shoulders. "I'm fine. They're fine. We went to the

University of Washington clinic. I take anti-retroviral medication. No AIDS symptoms. The doctors gave me a clean bill of health and six months' supply of meds when we left Seattle."

"Thank God. I've seen a lot of it." He kissed her on both cheeks, next the lips. Gently, then passionately with deep emotion. "You're so brave. We just have to be very careful. I still want to drink your blood, but I won't. You guys look sharp today. Designer jeans?"

"You bet, Sally's specials."

"Sounds expensive."

She turned, shook her head in disbelief, then saluted him. "You goose, Sally's is Salvation Army."

Kara was first with the clown, then Karla, who said, "Please make them the same."

The gypsy clown drew lips exaggerated in orange and black and eyes with huge white ovals. Red droplets dripped from each side of the mouth down the chin.

Kip said, "Whose blood?"

They all laughed. The pleasure and security of eternal vampire life outweighed its bloody dangers and risks. At least in this version.

"Thanks, Kip," Karla said. "This is more funner than we expected." She hugged him with her head on his stomach.

"Much more," Kara said.

Kip asked, "Ready to eat, or do you want to play softball and scare others?"

"Let's eat," Karen said. "Yum-yum."

Kara used both hands to imitate shoveling food into her mouth very fast. "Oh, Mom, we love free food."

Kip said, "That's not such a bad way for a mother to be." He put his arm around Karen and squeezed as they strolled together.

Kip nodded to many of the homeless and then shook hands with the head of the Neighborhood Coalition. "Thanks for coming. We appreciate it."

Cell phone to her ear, Karen's face sagged, reddened and her eyes turned to narrow slits. "Oh, no, not you again. Leave us alone. It's over. Don't follow…"

Kip grabbed the phone. "Stay away. I used to be a cop. Don't show up. Your time is finished with Karen."

Karen hugged him and kissed his hands. "You shouldn't have. You're wonderful."

The cloudy dawn drifted into a clear, blue-turquoise sky, ninety degrees with moderate humidity and breathable, windless air. Perfect picnic weather.

The accordion trio tuned up and began with a zydeco romp about bayou love in Louisiana. Karen and Kip danced briefly with energy, then all four joined the food line. The girls headed straight for desserts. Each plated chocolate cake, key lime pie, and a caramel apple. "Yummy," was all Kip heard.

Kip and Karen chose sliced turkey, meatloaf, green beans, corn-bread and lemonade. Karen said, "Who needs booze? Lemonade and vodka don't mix. Believe me, I know. Both of us in recovery is a no-no in twelve-step programs. Doesn't work very well in intimate relationships."

Kip said, "I know. Bill will not be a happy camper. For now, though, lemonade hits the spot!"

Kip walked near the hardcore homeless, among them, Queenie, Namey, and Buster, lounging on the ground or sleeping on blankets. They appeared lost, didn't know what to do with themselves, uninterested in softball, volleyball, hiking. Even chess and checkers didn't suit them. Without wine, drugs, or TV, most simply stagnated. Two volunteers circulated with Cokes and small chocolate bars. Kip felt pleased that Queenie behaved herself! Namey said, "Big shot now."

The homeless people didn't have much fun and simply didn't know what to do for fun. They did eat up a storm, locked into a survival mode, so by mid-afternoon all of the food was gone. Many carried away Styrofoam boxes or cups, food and goodies, never sure where the next meal would come from.

Kip strolled back to Karen, who said, "No leftovers for supper."

The girls ran off to fly kites with several other kids.

"Karen, I feel so good around you and the twins. You're all so wonderful and damn well adjusted."

She laid her hand on his thigh, pinched him lightly, then blew him a kiss. "The support, the kindness, you…it's heartwarming. I'm going to see a public defender, check into the divorce and see if I need a new permanent restraining order in Texas."

Kip said, "Good idea. I almost forgot to tell you. Two skinheads who think they're Nazis confessed to killing Squeaky. They bragged that they killed the wrong guy."

Karen nodded with sad, sympathetic eyes. "This world of ours."

The woman walking toward them took Kip by surprise. "Oh, my God, it's Marty." He ran to her and they embraced and hugged and kissed.

"Karen, this is Marty. Marty, Karen. Fantastic." His body tingled with pleasure. His face lit up, eyes bright and loving.

Marty said, "Hey, we're partners and parents. When you sent me the announcement of this party, I knew I had to be here." She hugged Kip again.

Karen said, "I've heard so many good things about you. It's nice to put a name with a face, and such a beautiful face, too."

Marty admired Karen, too. "Thanks. You guys look like an item." She pulled up a chair so she sat between them.

"Don't waste time, do you?" Kip said. "How's Roberto and your professor? I really miss him."

"More in love with both than I ever thought possible. I hope you'll see Roberto soon. Go to the zoo and enjoy the elephants. He loves elephants." Her arm dangled like a trunk hunting for peanuts.

Karen said, "Sounds like a great kid. I've got twins and a horrible soon-to-be ex-husband. We're separated. He's in Seattle."

Marty said, "A fresh start with Kip. Greatest guy who ever lived." She reached out to touch his arm. "Here come your girls."

"Mommy, can we play on the slides and swings with Tottie?" Karla said, tugging at Kara's hand.

"Oh, please, please, please!" Kara put her hands together prayerfully.

"No way, you two. Tottie's too old," Kip said.

"He is not," Karla said. She jumped up and down.

"Is it cause he's a street kid?" Kara said.

"No," Kip said, "it's because he's a bad influence. Sorry."

Tottie strode to Kip. "I'm sorry, Kip. Here's your backpack. It's all there."

Kip peeked inside. "Thanks, Tottie. I was fed up with you. It takes a big man to apologize."

Tottie stuck out his hand. Kip grabbed it, then hugged him. "Want me to help you? School, not a job on the street?"

"Yes, please, I need it. Then I can be a somebody like you."

Kip said, "Girls, go ahead and play with Tottie. I'll keep an eye on the three of you."

"Do as Kip says, girls," Karen said. "Fly your kites and play on the swings. Then we'll get ice cream." She high-fived with Kip as the girls trotted away with Tottie in tow. Kip followed them.

"There's going to be more music later. And a raffle of clothes, food, registration for job training and so on," Kip said. "Useful stuff. Raffle tickets are free. For a finale we're bringing in ponies for kids to ride."

"You know," Karen said, "I'm just stating the obvious, but it's nearly impossible to relax and have fun and enjoy yourself when you don't know where your next meal is coming from, or whether you'll have a bed for the night." She stood and rubbed Kip's shoulders.

"Beautiful and smart as hell, too," Marty said. "I want to take you both out to dinner later, and your girls too, if you like. Just took a good part-time job as an investigator, really a kind of spy, for a rich law firm. Undercover. Hush-hush stuff."

"Dinner sounds good. We'd love to," Kip said. He looked to Karen, who nodded and smiled.

Each woman gripped one of Kip's hands as they paraded through the crowd. Marty rose on her toes so she could whisper in Kip's left ear, "We want a baby girl. Will you?"

"Of course, but only the doctor's office with Playboy this time."

Marty said, "You do adore her, don't you?"

"A whole lot," Kip said, face flush with emotion.

Karen whispered in his other ear, "Me, too."

Kip's body throbbed with simple pleasure and fulfillment. His dual identity, the mutt, blended into a single, unified sense of himself, chest puffed out, eyes glistened, back straight and skin tingling. Blood pulsed through him, feeling more alive and worthwhile than he'd been in all the years since Wendy's death.

There was even a place for Marty, who joined the very first Homecoming Party in the park. Karen really opened up and trusted him. Tottie apologized and played safely with the girls. He hoped it was genuine. What a day! He was at peace with the world as he drove home.

Kip embraced Murphy's Law. He felt it, smelled it, suffered it, tasted it, and often prophesied it. Whatever can go wrong, will go wrong. He entered his apartment as the cell phone buzzed. He scrunched up his face, held his breath and closed his eyes, still hoping that this wonderful day wouldn't end. "Yes, it's Kip."

"Sir, this is the coroner, down on Main Street at the county building. I'm Dr. Singh. Met you once at the Landing."

"Sure, nice to talk to you." Nothing unusual so far, he told himself. Coroners and cops talk all the time.

"Well, Kip, I've got bad news. One of your regulars. They call him Namey."

Kip's heart beat faster and his breathing grew move shallow, as he awkwardly plopped down cross-legged on the floor. "What's happened?"

"Evidently your Homecoming Party in the park had ended. Most people left. It was just about dusk. Near the edge of the park where a few tall oak trees still stand. Must have been a drug deal."

"Yes, go on." He braced himself.

"Well, the way the cops got it. Namey and some other man got into an argument or a fight. Namey traded the guy some pills he had for meth. The other guy thought Namey cheated him and smashed his face several times with a tire iron. Namey bled out and was badly hurt, maybe he'd OD'd too, but he went berserk and stabbed the other guy with a pocket knife, right in the lungs and heart. Cops came. Namey threatened the cops with the knife. They shot him. Both guys are dead."

"Self-defense for Namey with the drug deal?"

"Cops think so, but the only witness is not very reliable," Dr. Singh said. "I remember Namey because he claimed the ashes, the remains, of his friend Squeaky who was burned to death. Didn't say anything."

"Yes. They were pals. Both Vets, different wars."

Dr. Singh said, "Sorry, Kip, but I've got to call Namey's doctor at the VA Clinic. Namey carried his card. His body shows more tracks than most."

Kip stared at his own AA card showing a list of meetings. There was an open night meeting he could catch in about an hour at the VA clinic. Now he sobbed. He cried for Namey, for Squeaky, for himself, for the world. He thought the goddamn fucking world is just too much for us. Way too much.

He had to try to help these people, but maybe it was just too goddamn much to expect. So much easier to arrest criminals and put them in jail. Just plug away, keep going, stay strong and all that good stuff. Another day ahead. Then another.

Chapter Fifteen

Kip spoke to the assembled one hundred or more Landing clients, now eager for their hot dinner. Once a week no one ate unless they first attended the meeting called "Center Court." They could stand or sit or sleep, as long as they showed up in the outdoor plaza. Just be there!

"Remember, we've got a jobs board, so put up your ad, and if you need help with it, my secretary or Karen will help you. Let me read several of them, so you get the idea. I circulate appropriate ads to employers and companies all over town. Job market is tough. This ad is anonymous, since I don't want to embarrass anyone. Ask yourself, would you hire this guy?"

He read: "You probably won't hire me since I still slip up. Drink wine and pass out and wake up and drink more wine. Before I start to drink I'm a good worker. I'm only thirty-two and I'm a white man and pretty darn strong and a good built. I can start work at 6 a.m., good until noon. Then I drink. I'll do any work. Had two years of high school but didn't learn much. Don't get along very well with other people. They cheat me. They want to change me. You know how it is. My middle initial is 'L.' Maybe life, or love. I'll work for food but I'd rather have red wine."

Enuf-el said, "We got to forgive and forget. We need to be a team. Care about each other." His huge body edged closer to the front, flashing his toothy grin while he patted the backs of some. "Who the hell will hire somebody like that? That's so damn honest. It hurts you."

Kip said, "The VA can't find work for this guy."

Kip read again: "I served in the infantry in Vietnam and got hit by shrapnel in my back. Had a lot of operations at the VA hospital. I can walk pretty good. Been living on the street for a lot of years. Getting along okay, but I want to work now. My social worker says I can work. So does my doctor. I'll do anything. Be a laborer or a truck driver. Drove truck in the Army. I'm sixty-one now. Please help me. Real cheap to start. Don't hold my age against me. Don't forget I fought off the Cong."

Karen said, "This guy is trying. Has a doctor and a social worker."

"That's right," Kip said. "Put your best foot forward in a job ad. Promote yourselves. At least let the employer know about treatment, or twelve-step, or that you are trying hard, getting some help working on problems."

Kip couldn't miss the restlessness in Center Court. People coughed and sneezed, plastic chairs scraped noisily, layers of clothing rustled, fingers trembled slightly in torn half-gloves. The crowd grew more jittery by the minute. They wanted dinner.

A tall man, a newcomer with a thick carrot-top and a long, red, untrimmed beard raised his hand. "I'll read what I said on mine, before I ripped it off the fucking job board.

"They said I should work now. Don't really want to. Almost finished college. Went to Iraq twice. So hot and dusty I could hardly breathe right. A bomb went off real close to me and I haven't been right since then. I can't think right or remember very well. I get real jumpy if I have to fill out papers. I tried meth in Iraq. I still use it when I have money. What the fuck."

Buster perched on his chair and did a slow, poorly balanced 360 degree turn. "Is that a job ad or do you just want attention? That won't get you a boss anywhere. Not even a winery."

Crowd applause and sustained laughter with cat-calls. Then a growing chant of, "Buster knows. Buster knows."

Kip said, "Well, Red, maybe you should try one of our job classes. They'll help you with a resume, employer contacts, and how to figure out what you want to do. Don't forget our drug services. Meth and jobs don't mix."

The chanting started again, "Let's eat. Let's eat. Let's eat."

Red said, "I guess all I really want is freedom. No job, no house, no wife and no kids. I just like the Declaration of Independence."

Kip said, "Come to the class, anyway. It's usually empty. You'll get a lot of individual attention and avoid the scams. Don't sign up for any home health treatments. That doesn't work at the Landing, even if they pay you."

"Shit, man. Nobody hires us. Especially if you're screwed up, like me," said Red. He spit tobacco juice on the ground, spattering the person squatting next to him. "Sorry. My aim ain't good. Believe it or not, I heard of a guy from here who firebombed the owner of a company that didn't hire him."

Again, "Let's eat. Let's eat. Let's eat."

"I'm not Moses," Kip said. "I just want to hear about any other problems or complaints." He held up his notepad and pen. "I'll keep a record."

"Do we have to be here?" Denty said. The packed outdoor plaza exploded in hoots and cheers. The aroma of pork ribs and baked beans tested their patience, but enticed all to remain. "No court, no dinner. I guess that's fair."

Kip said, "I agree."

Buster stood on his chair. "This life is hard. Maybe a wee drop or two to fight off the wind and chill." Laughter choked him. "Or this damn hot spell."

Kip moved near Buster. "There is a place. I think it's in Seattle, where you get an apartment and you can keep drinking. I'll look into it for you."

Buster jumped off the chair, ran to Kip and threw his arms around him. "Yesiree!"

Kip said, "Listen up, please. Don't forget we have alcohol and drug services. And AA and NA groups meet here several times daily. For those who choose to stop, and live one day at a time."

The tempting hints of dinner which wafted into the plaza from the nearby kitchen fought off the putrid odor of dirty clothes, unwashed bodies, and the plain, old-fashioned, salty sweat of Kip's flock. A draw.

When Buster puked all over himself, Kip nearly lost it. "Clean him up, please."

Queenie took off her mohair sweater, used it to soak up the mess and wiped Buster's shirt. "He's fine. Just fine," she said. "I've still got two layers over these." She jiggled her falsies playfully.

Kip's eye twitched. Then he raised his face to admire the setting sun through the trellis overhang. His prayerful hands turned into clenched fists. He said, "Our neighbors worry about a lot of things. Very few came to the picnic and party in the park. Just a handful."

Queenie said, "This damn city ain't Seattle. Wouldn't go for booze or drugs in homeless housing. They'd laugh their ass off. Scared to death some sex predator would grab a kid."

Kip said, "I'm afraid Queenie's got a point. That old warehouse, the one two blocks from here, is empty and would make a good place for housing after we spend a few bucks to fix it up. I've got the money and our board supports it, but that big daycare center on the block behind it says, 'No way, José,' to our plan. We just don't have enough money to pay big-time lawyers to fight them."

Tottie said, "I'm a kid. Nobody's ever bothered me at the Landing." He grinned proudly.

Reynaldo said, "Any way to reach Dock?"

"Not yet," Kip said. "Sorry."

Karen leaned on the building. She said, "We've got to be realistic. Two of our volunteers and their wives are dead. Two of our clients are dead. Squeaky and Namey. We're all worried."

Enuf-el spoke. "Let's eat. I'm hungry. Street people do shit, they'll steal, panhandle, even cut you." He rubbed his neck where the short, rippled scar healed. "But so do other people. They do shit. Plenty of it. Big-time banks. All that shit."

The crowd stood as one, cheering Enuf-el's words and his own personal bravery. "Eat. Eat. Eat."

"We have to remember our dead brothers and vets' housing. Another time we'll tackle issues like noise, crowding and the lack of cleanliness in the bathrooms," Kip said. "Tonight, before we get to the ribs and beans, we've got to honor Squeaky and Namey. Squeaky was murdered in cold-blood and Namey killed after he OD'd and went berserk with a knife. Two good vets, both had Purple Hearts, but also good hearts, for that matter." Standing applause with shouts of bravo. "They had no family, although they became buddies here. They won't be buried in pauper's graves, but the VA and military benefits don't provide much of a send-off."

Denty said, "Squeaky was real sick but Namey tried to beat his drug problem. Always tried hard." Tears rolled over her puffy cheeks onto her lips.

Queenie cradled Denty's head and shoulders and rocked slowly. Denty broke loose and stood in front of her chair. "That fucker Tony was a good man, too."

Kip said, "I'm going to take a new veteran's project to my Board of Directors and dedicate it to those vets we've lost. The Board will do something else for Tony and Rocco later."

Karen said, "Tell us about the project for vets."

Kip said, "I'll keep it short and simple. I'm just as hungry as the rest of you."

"Let's eat. Let's eat. Let's eat." Some folks lined up outside the cafeteria door.

"The idea is to build apartments as transitional housing," Kip said.

"Let's eat. Let's..."

"Hold it, please. This is different. It's better. Tenants pay part of the rent, but the rest of the rent is subsidized. The tenants, the vets, can have an equity interest in the project, actually own a piece of it. There are medical and mental health services and on-the-job training at the property. The founder of the project said, 'I trust most vets. I want them to succeed and rebuild their lives.'"

Silence from the crowd. Heads nodded. A few smiles. No one moved.

Kip said, "Let's eat." They moved quickly, as one, to the door when it opened. The homeless army travels on its stomach.

Kip ate with Karen seated next to him. He said, "We've got so much in common, it's scary. Black fathers. Booze. Sort of lost for the moment. In between. Wendy's gone. Your charming husband is finished."

Karen moved closer. "Does it make us too vulnerable, too ready to jump into things?"

"My dad died heartbroken over my brother. He was a good dad. Supportive, loving, encouraged school. I always felt mixed up, not sure if I was black or white or whatever. My identity always sort of on trial. I was light-skinned so I might have passed for white if I wanted to. Never did. Never had too. Felt like I'd betray them both."

She kissed him on the cheek. Then pecked his lips. Held his hands. "My parents met while dad was a soldier and my mother, a young Japanese girl, worked at the army base. My mother was fair-skinned for an Asian, so I ended up with almond eyes and a light-brown skin. Exotic, they say. More important, though, they got along beautifully. Sympatico. East and West merge, they used to say. My own white husband shocked me after we married. The booze and drugs set off his resentment and explosive outbursts. Sober, he was..."

Kip slid closer to her. He squeezed her hand.

"Ouch. Looser just a little."

He obeyed.

"That's perfect. Just perfect."

Kip wolfed down dinner, excused himself and went straight to his office. Energized by the needs and issues of his community, he also felt dragged down by their inconsistent performance and outright resistance. He typed out a provisional Op-Ed newspaper piece, a bit too long and wordy, but he'd prune it later and then e-mail it to his Board of Directors.

NEWSPAPER OP ED

"Homeless people scare us. They drive fear into us, anger us beyond acceptable frustration, and are thought to be without conscience, a sense of decency, or a citizen's normal responsibility. To the public, they appear to be outcasts, destitute, often uneducated and on the dole.

It's no secret that the gap between the haves and have nots is growing in our community. Breadwinners lose jobs and then parents and children live in poverty. Families represent a fast-growing homeless group. Homeless shelters or halfway-houses are not good places to raise kids, especially gay youth who've been abandoned by their parents.

The pain of a rootless status fuels much of the self-righteous pity for the homeless, though such compassion usually makes it someone else's problem to solve. Why not house them on the do-gooders' street, next to their fancy houses with swimming pools and foreign cars?

Countless arguments based on facts, homeless dwellings do not generally ruin communities or lower property values or lead to more violent felonies, prove useless. In good transitional housing the homeless are carefully screened for their ability to manage a more-or-less normal life in their own homes or apartments. They receive on-site services as needed. Remember that a ride to an AA meeting or hopping the bus to buy food is normal.

Many individuals think in concrete terms such as us and them, whenever crime, property values, or neighborhoods are mentioned. It's the in group versus the out group. Emotions like disgust and fear take over. Closer contact between us and them break down barriers and improve attitudes, both conscious and unconscious, about the growing number of homeless individuals and families."

Unable to sleep after he stopped typing, Kip paced his apartment, sorry that he'd dumped all of the bottles of wine and vodka. He shook with angst, trembling from an uncontrollable, nearly combustible sense of hope, edged with caution, compounded by futility.

These people, yes, most of them, his flock, the street people, those homeless working folks, simply down on their luck, or the ones who preferred their own painful versions of freedom and independence were more interested in feeding their bellies than solving their own problems, or helping with the issues of their compatriots. They wanted to survive, food and a shower and a bed. Or simply to be left alone to sleep in a doorway or cardboard box.

Kip suffered the frustration of wanting to help, but eagerly resisted by those most in need, or apparently so. He almost blurted out, "Let them eat cake," although that would have been more about him than them. The homeless had their reasons and every

145

right to refuse or avoid or deny assistance, even to have so little empathy for their mates.

Kip knew all too well the ups-and-downs inherent in one's personal struggles for maturity. Booze was one thing. Social life was another. No wife, with whom to grow old, and no kids, and his identity, always confused to some extent. And then his career path. It was so goddamned fucking hard to go one-day-at-a-time and stick with it. I could become an impossible burden.

He'd call Bill. He'd look deep inside himself after he returned from the upcoming conference in Houston.

Chapter Sixteen

Kip's eye twitched when he thought of Dock getting what he wanted from the Martinelli situation. A successful snitch, to say the least. According to the WPP grapevine, Dr. Ralph Meade morphed into Dr. Roger Morris, an adjunct professor of public administration at a local community college in Houston. He occupied a small one-bedroom apartment near the school, stuffed a closet with fishing tackle for use in the Gulf, and drove a two-year-old Japanese coupe. He dated the secretary from the college who was divorced with a young daughter.

The FBI did well by him, as he had enough money for a laid-back, apparently safe lifestyle. Not only had he sent Tony and Rocco and wives back to their maker and basically gotten away with it, he avoided punishment for his numerous other crimes. The murders represented just about as good a job as he could do on those rats.

Kip despised the malevolent, criminal, side of Dock, murder, theft, drugs, yet he grudgingly acknowledged Dock's efforts on behalf of the Landing, the useful and responsive part of his leadership.

Curiosity got the better of Kip, so he used his contacts in the Bureau to find Dock. When he traveled to Houston for a statewide homeless shelter directors' conference, the two met over lunch at a Mexican café near the campus and stuffed themselves with enchiladas full of meat and cheese and hot chilies.

Dock said, "Tony, eat your heart out. You never cooked like this."

Kip said, "Is WPP doing a good job for you?" He spit out a tiny green chili when he coughed up the heat. "You look different, at least."

"My long, brown hair parted in the middle and the horn-rim glasses give me a preppie, professional, look, don't you agree?"

Dock said, "It's hotter than hell here. A wet sauna but I'm safe. WPP has been great."

Kip said, "A safe and secure rat who jumped ship."

"That's it. I should hate myself but I don't. That Mafioso earned it. He's a killer." Dock cleared his throat and wiped the sweat from his brow.

Kip said, "You're also a fucking killer, and a thief and a drug dealer, and you're on the street. Shitty justice system. You deserve life." He threw his napkin to the floor, then bent over to pick it up and shake it forcefully. "In a prison cell, that is."

Dock pursed his lips to muffle a smug laugh, but his wide mouth and bright eyes gave him away. "Take it easy. Such an angry idealist, Kip. Plea bargain. Just like food stamps and Social Security and Medicare. Government helps its own."

"What did you do with the gun?" Their unblinking gazes locked.

Dock hemmed and hawed and then said, "You know we had all the homeless folks and the staff patted down for guns or knives, even box cutters, each time they entered the gate at the Landing. Any weapons confiscated were then burned and destroyed in a police furnace outside of town. No serial numbers, photographs, or drawings of these weapons, just obliterated in a high-intensity furnace designed for that purpose. Believe it or not, our weapons were destroyed together with batches from the police department's evidence room. I'm not saying that's what I did with the gun, but I'm not saying I didn't, either." He closed his eyes, opened them and glanced at shadows on the floor.

A hot sun flooded the restaurant patio as they drank sweet iced tea to calm the spicy chilies. Sunlight shone directly on Dock's face like a low-hanging bare bulb during a routine police interrogation.

Kip's scar heated up, became thick and itched. He said, "You're a very savvy guy, Professor Morris. Got even with a couple of snitches. Very cool."

"Yes, I'm fine with it. I'd had enough of the Landing. Too much violence. Never safe there. Always on my guard."

"By the way," Kip said, "when the hospital discharged Enuf-el, he decided not to press assault charges against the two others. He said they were his buddies. He forgave them."

Dock said, "I saved his life. Oh, I wanted to thank you for alerting me to the concerns about WPP in Houston. Your phone call. I've taken extra precautions. A guy followed me, or so I thought a few weeks ago. Maybe I'm just getting paranoid in my old age." He stirred and sipped his tea.

"Good," Kip said. "You're resourceful as hell." They clinked glasses in a toast that neither one really meant.

"And you, Kip, I envy you. You've got Karen and her girls, my informants tell me. And you're doing a great job. Of course, there's your little booze problem and that lesbian on the down side. Gay women..."

Kip slipped an envelope out of his shirt pocket. He handed it to Dock. "I'll overlook your last bullshit. Here's Tottie's report card. I'm sure he'd want you to see it. The teacher says, 'Shows real promise.' How about that?"

Dock nodded and he rolled his eyes, blue-changed-to-green with new contacts. "You've taken my spot in more ways than one. He's a kid, just a kid. He probably forged the report card. I miss him. He was one of my mules and street salesmen."

Kip said, "You really are a first-class asshole."

Dock sighed as his face sagged. He blew out a moan. "I'm glad it's all out in the open. It's a relief. The murders, the drug deal, prison. Even the small stuff like the cash at Sally's and the truckload of food at the Soup Kitchen. I've done a bunch of things for the feel of it, the chance to get away with it, defy the world, prove my cleverness. I'm not a guilty guy seeking sympathy. I never want punishment again. I even had a plan to sell kids over the internet. Then you came along."

He paused and stood. His leg buckled and he grabbed the back of his chair. "The stress and strain were horrible, since I had to hide important aspects of my life, things about my background and lifestyle that no one knew, or even considered likely for a man like me with that Ph.D. degree. The stolen federal-grant money and the phony information used to get student loans. I thought I could beat any system, never get caught, but if I did I'd be protected and helped in a cover-up. In Dallas I was always being someone I wasn't. That's the price of my life…the joy and the cost of it all."

Kip's eye twitched. He pushed back his chair and faced Dock. "Yeah, but you were always being someone you shouldn't be. That's why you had to cover it up, and be someone you weren't. Same thing now and the FBI is hiding the real you. The killer."

"You're still a cop at heart. If you didn't have me, you couldn't protect and serve." Dock created a pistol out of his right hand.

"At least I'm a compassionate cop. You get credit for being clever and energetic, but naïve as hell, all in the service of…"

"Why spend time with me? My evil hides inside my good. I helped homeless people and used them for my own purposes. Criminal purposes. You hide plenty yourself, but you don't know it. Mr. Nice Guy and all that tree trimming bullshit." He hummed a few bars of "Silent Night."

Kip paid the bill and they strolled slowly out of the café into the bright sunlight. Kip rubbed his eyes without taking off his new Ray-Bans. "Must be the humidity down here. Not Christmas yet, but here's your present. Some good things have happened at the center lately. We've started a series of Homecoming Parties in the park, so the homeless can learn to enjoy themselves and have fun. Then Karen made an impassioned plea for new transitional housing at a community meeting."

"It's all behind me now. I'd like to show you my office at the campus," Dock said.

"A brief visit. Where did you get that limp? I've always been curious," Kip said.

"Well, some guy started a rumor in prison that I was a child molester. Two guys knifed me in the chest and the thigh. They sewed me up at the infirmary but left me with a limp. Something about a tendon sliced. Not the Mayo Clinic."

Kip said, "I got my knife thing from a perp I finally tackled, after chasing him all over hell. He cut my face pretty bad. Then I shot him. Only kill on my record as a cop." He gently patted the furrowed scar.

Dock said, "Don't turn around. There's a black BMW. I've seen it earlier this week. Guy with big, dark sunglasses and an Astros baseball cap. Drives a bit and then just parks and waits and tries to look innocent."

Kip dropped his keys and turned around to peek as he reached for them. "Yes, I see him. Dark skin. Big nose. Middle-age."

"Let's cross the greenbelt here and see what happens. Cars are prohibited in this area." Dock clumsily picked up the pace as he led the way.

"They want you, Dock. You know that. Witness Protection can be a secure, safety net, usually it is, but at times it's just a sieve and info leaks all over the place. Wiseguys would pay a fortune to find you. That would be the end of it. Boom! I'd hate to see that happen."

"Why the hell do you care?"

"Good question." Kip shrugged and shook his head. "I'm not sure. Maybe it's because I'm screwed up in my own way. Maybe it's because you did some good things at the Landing. I'm just not sure. It's something."

Dock said, "Lousy answer. I repeat, Why help me? You hate murderers. You've got the heart of a cop. I'm the bad guy." Selfish pride in his eyes and a smug sneer on his narrowed lips.

Kip said, "I know you are. I wouldn't mind you frying for those murders. But I wouldn't mind assisting you, either. Go figure." He shook his head slowly in sheer disbelief of his own ambivalence.

"Keep walking. Ready for a shocker?"

"Go ahead." Kip's eye twitched in anticipation.

Dock said, "We're brothers. Half-brothers. Same mother. My mom and your dad had a very brief, drunken fling. You're the result. Black father and white mother, so you're a light brown mixed breed."

Kip stayed cool on the outside, a turbulent stew on the inside. "Did my own mother know? I didn't. No one ever told me. I was always Kip Crandall, plain and simple."

Shock suddenly settled in. Head bowed, Kip kneeled in the sunlight, unable to continue walking. "You're the real bastard. I'm not illegitimate, my biological father raised me."

"You are, but who cares? We're brothers. I'm not sure who knew what or when, but our mother gave you up to your own mom and dad. She never looked back. Your father took you as an infant." Dock smiled triumphantly, "So that's why you always had me in your craw. I'm your other half. You said you'd help me, that you wanted to warn me, so that I wouldn't be killed. So that my back would be covered. Blood is thicker than water." He limped ahead as Kip got to his feet again.

Kip's mind reeled with this horrifying information and Dock's filthy insinuations. His mother, Dock's mother, and his father. Too much to process quickly. Way too much. The scar became nearly unbearable. He said, "You've lied all your life. Kept secrets. Covered up. Never been who you say you are. I don't believe a word of this bullshit. I should probably kill you right now and save the Feds a lot of money. You deserve it. You're a fucking rat! Rats don't live long!"

Dock said, "Our mother swore it's the truth. We're brothers."

Kip thought he could go to the hospital birth records, but if his dad was the father then they probably covered up the mother's true name. His parents were dead. They'd been good to his brother and him. Wonderful parents. Loving, supportive, responsive and tried to solve problems together.

What's the difference now? A fling? So what? At least they didn't dump him in an orphanage or adopt him out to a complete stranger. Fuck it. He'd figure it all out later. It did have the ring of truth. Dock couldn't gain much at this point with such an outrageous lie. Kip was already trying to warn him and try to get him to take his situation more seriously, to be more careful, and less trusting. The watchful eye of a brother!

Low-lying fluffy white clouds hid the sun for a moment. Blue sky and bright sunlight quickly reappeared. They crossed the greenbelt area, filled with plenty of drought-resistant plants, mostly Johnson weed, and crepe myrtle with red flowers.

The same BMW parked on the street near their destination, a group of new campus buildings. Different driver though, this time a blonde man in his twenties whose long hair hung below a black chauffeur's cap.

"So damn hard to know," Dock said. "Maybe WPP guys on surveillance."

"Don't take any chances." Kip took off his sunglasses and glanced at Dock. "Don't take any chances. Call WPP and tell them."

"I promise. Thanks, Mother," Dock said. "Just because I'm paranoid, that doesn't mean I'm wrong."

"It's up to WPP to find out. Their job."

The campus tour revealed molded concrete, low-slung modern two-story buildings, freshly landscaped and well-maintained. Students in their mid-twenties and thirties, loaded down with backpacks and computer cases lumbered slowly along the wide walkways.

"It's all green and wheelchair accessible, see the ramps?" Dock said.

"Yes, yes," Kip said. "Very functional and impressive. Wait till the trees and shrubs mature. It'll be even more attractive." He'd calmed down, breathing slower and heart rate close to normal.

They entered a Frank Lloyd Wright-inspired office building and walked up one flight of stained concrete stairs to an office door with "Dr. Morris" on it. The building smelled of new construction, dusty with an A/C system that hummed.

"Home, sweet, home," Dock said. "You know, they'll never get me. I'm smart, educated, and the FBI has my back." He pulled the blinds on an overly small, double-pane window that looked out on the campus and parking lot. "You're welcome to come to my 2:00 p.m. class on nonprofit management. You could even be a guest speaker."

"Some other time."

"Speaking of the next time," Dock said, "we'll fish offshore in the gulf. Catch some big trophies." He pretended to cast with a fishing rod. "Sooner or later, the hatred and the booze and the drugs, the stink, too, will wear you down, probably wear you out. You'll feel like hiding. You'll see there's a bad guy inside you somewhere."

"You really are a bastard. Honest in a funny way and all that, but a real bastard. There's plenty of tension and stink when we're together." He knew his scar reddened when it itched horribly, but he didn't give in to it. Instead, he reached to pat his holster and gun, an old habit. He no longer carried it.

Dock cleaned his brown horn rims with his tie, then placed the sunglass lenses into their case. "You got Karen. And her kids. You always wanted my job. You'll never understand kids like Tottie."

"I win. You lose. That's it."

Dock grabbed Kip's wrist, held tightly, and twisted. He dropped it as Kip winced in pain. "Don't forget me," he said.

His phone chimed. "Hello, this is Professor Morris. Yes, this is Morris. These damn cell phones. The line cut out. Maybe an unhappy student or a market researcher."

"Got to run. Good luck. Be vigilant. The FBI is not leak-proof," Kip said.

"See you, Kip. I've always had a kind of faith in others. Whenever I did anything questionable as a kid, shoplifting or lying, my two sisters defended me at home. I took some candy from a store when I was about ten or eleven years old, and they even made me give it back. Somebody had my back. Now you do."

Kip left. He abruptly stopped midway down the stairs. Had he heard a 'pop,' the sound of an automatic pistol with a silencer? He turned on his heels and ran back to Dock's office and knocked. No answer.

He entered and found Dock lying face down behind his desk, one small bullet hole in the back of his skull. Head turned slightly to the side, face smeared with brains and bone and blood, the finality of a death rattle.

There was no pulse. Kip turned him onto his back and performed CPR. He broke off to call 911, then resumed. Still no response. Difficult, nearly impossible to shoot yourself in the back of the head like this. No gun and no bullet casings, so the impossible suicide became a homicide certainty. A huge, stinking, dead, black rat, à la New York City garbage, dangled from Dock's desk lamp. Mafia justice.

Kip said, "You dumb fuck. It was only a matter of time. You were too hot to handle."

The EMTs arrived and continued resuscitation attempts using

CPR, then paddles, and finally injections directly into the heart. Dock, Roger Morris, alias Ralph Meade, aka Rod Mulligan was dead.

Kip examined the office after the EMTs returned their equipment to the ambulance. With no chance Dock could be revived or saved in the emergency room by a physician, he'd be pronounced dead by the county medical examiner.

Kip pointed out where he found Dock on the office floor to two street cops, and then to the detectives. They roped off the whole office and the hallway as the crime scene.

At least the EMTs didn't cover their asses by rushing Dock's body to the ER.

Kip reasoned that the hit man must have known the building and office set-up, probably been in and out several times. He apparently knew the exit door location, the rear stairway, and the rooftop. The phone call told him Dock's location, then he moved fast and 'pop.'

Benedetto was avenged. Alive, he might say, "Young hit men move fast, but old hit men know the way. Mafioso rules!"

Later, Kip explained to the detectives that he had been at lunch with Dock, then they walked back to campus. He vaguely recalled a late-model black SUV drive by several times, but assumed it was simply someone looking for a parking space. Then he remembered an old guy in gray overalls and a white beard cleaning the hall floor.

He dialed the unlisted number of the Witness Protection Program in Houston and reported the details of what had happened. He provided a brief statement after identifying himself and Dock. They thanked him. The agent said, "We're supposed to call his mom, Eloise Mulligan in St. Louis." WPP Houston then went on total lockdown, fearing that the identity of others had been compromised.

Perhaps Dock could have partly redeemed himself if he had lived out his life, and made a worthwhile contribution as a professor and mentor. His penchant for danger and excitement cried out for control. The temptation to return to crime, to bolt WPP required Dock's vigilant resistance. Alone on the street he would have been a walking dead man, no one to cover his back. In the end, even the FBI program failed to protect him against a mob hit.

While Kip flew back to Dallas, he worked out a plan to tell Tottie about Dock's death in baby steps. Emphasizing his positive attributes without skipping over some of the negatives. Dock and Tottie cared about each other in their own way, just as Kip and Tottie did. Kip decided to make sure Tottie carried some kind of ID card out on the streets. He'd teach him to be more cautious. No more sagging pants, oversized shirts, or sideways baseball caps.

Kip's early life taught him to be protective toward his brother and mother. Those lessons carried over into his confusing and uncertain relationship with Dock. Strangely, he felt that they were almost two sides of the same coin, whether they were brothers or not.

He asked the flight attendant for a third vodka on the rocks. He missed the olives. He stuffed his mind full of loving thoughts of Karen and the twins. In their own home someday soon, a comfortable family van, maybe a couple of peaceful dogs and homework. Plenty of homework, so these girls would achieve something meaningful in life. Karen would be proud. He would be proud. His parents would be proud. So would Eloise Mulligan of St. Louis.

REVENGE TRILOGY By Norman Giddan

The Bogus Killer
A transsexual hides several murders behind a smokescreen of exaggerated and fanciful false confessions of serial killings, including cannibalism and dismemberment. PI's Kip and Marty get to the truth after many wrong turns.

The Rat Murders
Kip and Marty track down the lurid criminal past of Dock, head of a homeless shelter. A felon who rats out his former prison cellmate, he is murdered, and Kip replaces him. Kip and Dock share an unusual relationship.

Coming Soon! *The Investigator*
(with Jamel J. Jones and Martin Longoria)
Graphic novel in which Kip and Marty bat their heads against the wall to discover what's behind the seemingly related massacres of rabbis, priests, and evangelists. Coincidence? Government agency? Muslim radical extremists?

From Cult Classics Publisher of Dallas
Available on Amazon.com
In print and as e-books